CIRCLING TOWARD NIGHTFALL

CIRCLING TOWARD NIGHTFALL

A NOVEL

DENNIS MUST

• • •

ILLUSTRATIONS

RUSS SPITKOVSKY

Red Hen Press | *Pasadena, CA*

Book design by Mark E. Cull
Book layout by Ava Morgan

Library of Congress Cataloging-in-Publication Data

Names: Must, Dennis, author. | Spitkovsky, Russ, illustrator.
Title: Circling toward nightfall: a novel / Dennis Must ; illustrations
  Russ Spitkovsky.
Description: First edition. | Pasadena, CA: Red Hen Press, 2025.
Identifiers: LCCN 2025021045 (print) | LCCN 2025021046 (ebook) |
  ISBN 9781636282848 (paperback) | ISBN 9781636282862 (library binding) |
  ISBN 9781636282855 (ebook)
Subjects: LCGFT: Novels.
Classification: LCC PS3613.U845 C57 2025 (print) | LCC PS3613.U845
  (ebook) | DDC 813/.6—dc23/eng/20250512
LC record available at https://lccn.loc.gov/2025021045
LC ebook record available at https://lccn.loc.gov/2025021046

The National Endowment for the Arts, the Los Angeles County Arts Commission, the Ahmanson Foundation, the Dwight Stuart Youth Fund, the Max Factor Family Foundation, the Pasadena Tournament of Roses Foundation, the Pasadena Arts & Culture Commission and the City of Pasadena Cultural Affairs Division, the City of Los Angeles Department of Cultural Affairs, the Audrey & Sydney Irmas Charitable Foundation, the Meta & George Rosenberg Foundation, the Albert and Elaine Borchard Foundation, the Adams Family Foundation, Amazon Literary Partnership, the Sam Francis Foundation, and the Mara W. Breech Foundation partially support Red Hen Press.

First Edition
Published by Red Hen Press
www.redhen.org

CIRCLING TOWARD NIGHTFALL

PART ONE[1]
THE BEREA CANTICLE

1 Adapted from "Circling Toward Nightfall," short fiction originally published in *The Saint Ann's Review*, Brooklyn, NY, 2014 Issue, and *Oh, Don't Ask Why*, stories by Dennis Must, Red Hen Press, Los Angeles, CA.

"Characters buried alive in the mind . . ."

PRELUDE

The women in town adored the man as much as I did.

"What should I bring along?" I asked.

"Nothing. Food and drinks are included in the price. We'll have a terrific time."

Always the promise.

He'd bought us junket tickets for a baseball game in Cleveland under patronage of the Diamond—an eating and drinking tavern inside Berea's Old Penn Hotel. We were to congregate on the town's square and board a retired Greyhound bus at nine that Sunday morning. A halcyon day, passengers palavered and laughed to friends and strangers—mostly about how Ralph Kiner, home run ace, was fail-safe to dispatch Bob Friend to the showers in early innings. Whitey, the Diamond's head bartender, fetched bottles of beer from iced twenty-gallon galvanized garbage cans. Sandwiches wrapped in wax paper sat alongside in peck baskets.

A half-hour into the three-hour diesel-fumed journey, rhythmic applauding ignited in the seats. "Hey, isn't it story time? What say you, Billy Coombs?"

"Later," he pled. "Plenty of time," and squeezed my arm, murmuring, "Billy Coombs, their burlesque man. Give me a rest. I wish they'd let me be, kid."

He waved off the beer and shared a ham and cheese with me.

We arrived at the Indians' ballpark without incident—except for one reveler who paced the bus, exclaiming, "Behold the *Fontana di Trevi* Gardens any second now if this goddamned driver don't stop soon!" When our vehicle pulled onto the shoulder of the highway, even women scurried off into the brush.

* * *

But the Pirates lost badly that day. Bob Friend denied Pittsburgh's superstar even a measly base on balls. And with it, Billy Coombs's resolve to be a gentleman he began pissing away on the dour trip home. Where a goodly number of the excursion party wanted to sleep, he and a couple of his cronies took to polishing off the remaining bottles of warm beer.

"Hey!" Billy bellowed from the front of the bus. "So the highest paid Major League player didn't get it off today. Who among us ain't been there, huh?" he cracked, grasping his crotch, eyeballing those watching him. "Did you all just come to drift off in Morpheus's arms?" he taunted. "Rise up, Pirates!" As if they wouldn't, Billy Coombs would suddenly expire.

Bodies had slumped into their seatmates' laps. Whitey shrugged as if arousing the passengers was a lost cause. Billy returned to our seat warbling "My Melancholy Baby." A woman in front of us pitched her henna head to the bus's ceiling and wailed inconsolably, *"Now don't feel blue . . ."*

A handful of riders halfheartedly joined in, weeping in the suds they'd already quaffed—the now-empty garbage pails sloshing water in accompaniment.

I adored Billy Coombs at the outset of our trip that Sunday morning. In the owl light of day, I wished I hadn't come.

On the itinerary as the halfway-home leisure stop, the driver detoured to the Ukrainian Hall outside Stroudsville, Pennsylvania. We filed into a turreted Norman armory's cavernous assembly hall that promptly miniaturized our busload. A lone jukebox sat in one corner, a virtual football field away, amidst an island of vacant chromium dinette sets. In front of an empty dais, pre-cooked hotdogs lay in a metal warming box.

"We got to get home to the kids," several women groused. "Where's the toilet?"

Except Billy and his in-front-of-the-bus confederates were in a mood to party. "The Polish women here are hot!" one wheezed.

I only smelled disinfectant.

"Blue Moon" caddied up to the jukebox needle. Three inebriants waltzed onto the dance floor that was illuminated by light filtering through the armory's clerestory. Without glancing about for a willing partner, the revelers twirled in dazed stupefied motion.

"I saw you standing alone . . ."

But Billy Coombs, bathed in its gaseous rainbow, slumped against the Wurlitzer looking forlorn.

Numbed by fatigue and boredom, several of the party dropped

their heads on the Formica tables. Others sat smoking, waiting stoically in the nickel-plated light. Sunday evenings were always this way in the Rust Belt. One Diamond waitress blew bluish-gray rings into the armory sky.

"*The evening breeze caressed the trees . . . tenderly.*"

Faux palms aproned the shadowy stage.

I sensed Billy chafing under the waning light and its daybreak promise when unexpectedly he swanned into the midst of the three gyrators, who obligingly spiraled around him.

"*When you and I came wondering by, and lost in the stars were we.*"

He tapped the back of one Ernest Tyner, an Ichabod Crane type with a pronounced baritone voice, a gentleman not given to maudlin exhibition like his two companions. Yet he was often seen in their company . . . affirming their mutual resistance to flicker out like the ebbing light now enveloping them.

Ernest braked and opened his embrace wide. Billy Coombs, at least a foot shorter, sprang, and scissored his legs and arms about the man's reedy torso. Ernest broadened his span, aping the wings of the wooden eagle hovering above the armory's proscenium arch.

"*My heart goes where the wild goose goes!*" Frankie Lane debuted in the jukebox.

Now a pair of singles and one twosome eddied about the hall like moths of autumn.

It all appeared so normal . . . though a lady wouldn't have clung to Ernest Tyner so indelicately in public. In the dusky armory's far corner, a glint of skylight illuminated Billy Coombs like he was clinging to the yard of a mast, the whirling Ichabod. An Albert Ryder vessel caught in a summer tempest, a young boy's maelstrom—mine—watching his father *man-circling toward nightfall*.

* * *

Of late I've been awakening to the memory of the pair blithely orbiting the dance floor as dusk shrouds the armory's clerestory. Not one of the awake passengers appears at all surprised or jiggered by Billy and Ichabod's prelude to night. Episodes like this were the coin of excursions . . . the return trips home to the mill towns before their coach's earsplitting blast signals it's time to leave.

Except what I palpably recall of this tipsy cavort is a prickly longing and void that late Sunday afternoon once the oxygen had escaped the promise of the burlesque man and I sharing the day together.

Aching to embrace Billy's trunk as he had Ichabod's, I watched the twosome spinning away from me and feared being swallowed by the armory's stygian gloom. That he and Ernest were another star gamboling off into the shadowy ceiling, and I was left to join the blank-face riders awaiting the Greyhound's summons. That one man clinging onto another for dear life was levitating away from the assembled dead, rising above Ohio Valley's Sunday graveyard . . . escaping its pull of ennui and malaise.

Nights I even fancy myself charging after the pair, but am dissuaded by the anesthetized passengers who barely raise their heads, the smokers with their jaundiced eyes.

The kid will never catch up with the whirling duo, they mutter.

As if the homebound perceive that some men are dancers born to transcend darkness. To whirl about on the world's illusory stage.

That's just how it is.

Yeah, sure your old man loves you. Have another ham sandwich, kid. They're a bit stale by now. Here, put some catsup and relish on it. Do you want a soda?

Come back to the bus with us.

You won't tell your ma, will you?

That's Ernie "Ichabod" Tyner. He's a dipper like your old man at the pottery. Quite a stepper, too, don't you agree?

That's how we keep the light on, kid.

Can't take any of this life seriously.

Billy Coombs don't.

CHAPTER ONE

Ernest Tyner was the most religious man I knew.

If truth be told, a few believed he was Christ's son who lived among us. Even a couple of my boyhood friends swore *"Ichabod rose from the dead."*

Each morning before heading off to school I'd watch him walk down our street to catch the bus. *"Where does the son of Christ work?"* I wondered.

Word from the morning passengers was that he got off at the last stop and wandered out County Line Road alone. Except nothing was out there except the defunct dam whose water had been drained a century earlier and now was largely invisible in a forest of ailanthus and hickory trees. Over the years, the dam's one-hundred-foot concrete wall became our burg's jumping off place for mortally depressed residents. Hardly a year passed that two or three hadn't slogged out there with nothing on their backs but, say, a flowered housedress or a Sunday suit of clothes. No one tried to interfere, never raising their eyes above the black macadam roadway.

But when Ichabod walked down County Line Road each morning, he always returned as he had set out, impeccably dressed in a blue-serge double-breasted suit, starched white shirt, and a silk bloodred tie . . . same shade as his socks. His wing-toed bluchers shined mirror finish. Just how one might imagine the male offspring of the Lamb of God to fit into our mill town community.

And not unlike those woods that took root around the abandoned dam, so too the belief that Ichabod Tyner traveled down County Line Road each weekday to succor the deceased. That Christ's son did live among us. His day job was to minister to the afflicted. The dead who were deprived of DiCarlo's black Cadillac hearse with flower car cortege and long drive to Longview Cemetery of white salt-lick tombstones.

It only seemed right.

* * *

I wasn't sure why it happened.

My father, Billy Coombs, like everyone else on our street, acted as if he didn't see Ernest when he walked by one daybreak, and was surprised when Ichabod said "Good morning." I witnessed it all from inside the screen door.

Father muttered the same and reflexively snuffed out his cigarette on the sidewalk.

"I'm Ernest Tyner, your up-the-street neighbor."

Billy stood up, stiff as a doorpost. *Was he about to be asked to confess his countless sins?* It was a given that we all had them in abundance. They grew naturally like flies on mangy dogs of which there were legions in our neighborhood.

Ichabod didn't break a smile.

"I am Billy Coombs."

Ichabod stepped closer. "I understand you work at the pottery mill. That you have been a dipper there for several years. Is that correct?"

Billy nodded that it was.

"Well, it seems I'm no longer needed in my vineyard, and I was wondering . . ."

Vineyard's a biblical expression, mused Billy. *Is he referring to his ministering to the ghosts of the despondent on County Line Road?*

"Permit me to come right out with it, Mr. Coombs."

"Billy, please."

Still no Ichabod smile.

"I need a job," Ernest confessed like he was ashamed.

"They are hiring in the kiln room," Billy said. "Go to the guard house outside the plant and tell the foreman, Joe Bannister, that Coombs sent you. I'm sure it will go well."

Ichabod bowed back and forth like he did at Mass, thanking my father profusely. And sauntered back down the street.

Would we hear a keening rise up from the ailanthus and the hickory woods? I wondered.

"Jesus, did you catch all that?" flummoxed Billy stepping back into our living room. How do I explain it at the plant?"

But nobody asked him.

The following Monday morning Ernest joined my father at the bus stop and they both ended up sitting together in the first seat. Neither of them exchanging one word. Same at the quitting bell time as they headed home and climbed our street to their respective homes.

No "See you tomorrow." Not even a goodbye gesture.

And Billy would never talk about the nature of their relationship when I asked him about it. "You never asked him if he likes his new job? Sure as hell the men tease him about his height. He mentions that, right?"

Like Billy didn't hear me.

"Boy, your old man has finally found religion?" a wag at the local gas station jeered. "He gonna accompany Ichabod to St. Andrew's boneyard? Messiah's son sure as hell takes the sting out of its cold graves." Then raucous laughter would ensue, the local hangers-on joining in the chorus.

But Ichabod and Billy bonded like two mutes on those diurnal trips to and from the pottery mill.

* * *

I couldn't ask my mother, as I didn't have one . . . or that's what Billy always told me. Any one of those women he'd periodically bring home from Piesto's Bar at the end of our street late of a Friday night could have been she. If I was still up, I'd search their faces for a signal of motherly affection.

Mostly what I'd get in return was another kind that sent me to bed with wet dreams.

Billy and me. And now an Ichabod Christ on work days.

'Cause I'd begun to take to Ernie in the strange way Billy had. Like he and I had become steadfast friends. Except we never acknowledged as much to each other. Like Ichabod Christ was Billy's and my double.

One cold winter night after the second year of Ernie's employment, when Billy was smoking and reading the newspaper, I said I wanted to ask him something.

"What is it, kid?"

"What say we invite Ichabod to dinner one of these nights?"

Billy thought it hilarious, and near caught his pants on fire when he spit his cigarette out. "Oh, Jesus, yes! What will we feed him? Owl soup? Or we'll start off with a course of St. Andrew communion wafers slathered with horseradish. Fermented Holy Water to wash them down. Then you can serve him your dear mother's pasta recipe while I engage him in conversation. Christ, won't that be fun!"

"Do you suppose he plays gin rummy?" I asked.

"With a deck of Rosary Prayer Cards . . . maybe."

Our niggardly exchange was over for yet another night.

Perhaps I'd recognize Mother come Friday.

* * *

On my ninth Easter, Billy took me downtown and parked the car, a 1936 black Dodge sedan with mohair seats. We walked several blocks almost to the burg's limits when we came upon a block of two-story soot-stained stone row houses. The second residence from the very end, we walked up one flight of narrow stairs and knocked on the door. From inside a quaking voice, "Who is it?"

"Franz's brother," Father replied.

Several minutes passed until the brass doorknob turned. Standing there in the afternoon dark, as the window shades were down, stood a barely erect wizened snow-white-haired woman in a sackcloth nightdress.

"Billy!" she cried. "And who is this?" She ran her fingers across my face like she was blind.

"Franz's son."

She looked confused through her bottle lens eyeglasses.

Billy laughed. "Mamma, I'm kidding you. This is Jeremiah. Say hello to your grandmother."

"Happy Easter," I replied.

"Where's Pap?" Billy asked.

"Out dancing," she confided, before crawling back into her bed which occupied at least three-quarters of the room. She continued to grin at me and beckoned me closer. "Jeremiah, there is something in that bottom drawer for you to see. Go open it for me."

A shiny black chest of drawers stood at the foot of Grandma's bed.

I got down on my knees. Inside were three tarnished silver trophy cups. I could make out the etched Coombs name on each. But it wasn't Billy's.

"Those were won by your Uncle Franz who's a Monsignor. Our town's tennis champion when he was a grown boy. Wasn't he, Billy?"

Father was sitting in the room's bleakest shadow in a straightback wooden chair. He didn't utter a word or make a single gesture.

I lifted one of the trophies and handed it to her. "Where is Uncle Franz now?" I asked, having never been informed that I *had* any relatives.

Grandma stared at Billy for an answer.

"Sewickley," he muttered, standing up like it was time to go.

"Oh, it's too soon," she pled. "Can't you stay a little longer?"

Billy Coombs edged to the apartment's door.

"But it's Easter, Son," she protested.

"Franz's busiest day of the year, right?" Billy shoved the trophy door shut with his foot. The one lying alongside her in bed mirrored a ray of sun that had escaped from the window blind. The fiery yellow circle traveled aimlessly across the peeling ceiling.

"Goodbye," she said, with a slight wave to me. "You must come again without your father so we can spend time together. You might even meet your grandfather, if we're lucky."

It was the old woman's liquid blue eyes magnified behind those thick viscous-like lens that I couldn't escape for the remainder of that Easter day. It felt as if she were examining my heart. That those eyes would trail me home.

Several weeks later when school let out, I walked to town and climbed those steps to their flat.

It was that very late afternoon when I discovered who my mother was.

"Her name was Bernadette, Jeremiah."

"Where is she?"

"She left us in childbirth."

* * *

I distinctly remember the light rose shade of the walls in my room, the pine door with its shiny brass knob, the uncovered single double-pane window that taught me about the seasons. There was the ivory-colored crib in which I lay with its imposing side rails. But most vivid of all was the woman who cared for me those first years.

She wore a loose-fitting nut-brown tunic that draped her entire body and fell to the ground. A scarlet-red apron hung from both front and back of her neck. A stiff snow-white headpiece that coifed her face sequestered her hair. Attached was a starched bib that clung to her chin and fell board-like midway to her breasts. A black cloth veiled the headpiece while exposing her face and enveloping her shoulders. Gathering her tunic at her waist was a belt of hand-knotted white rope.

Each daybreak I awaited for her to enter my room.

As if in a dream, she would embrace me close to her scarlet-red apron. In all our encounters she never once uttered one word. But it never seemed to matter to me. It was her hazel eyes that spoke words that to this day I have no means to transcribe. When it was cold outside, she would swath me in the folds of her tunic and traverse a well-trodden path we had made through the woods surrounding the house where I assume I was born.

My favorite memory was her red scapular sweeping the newly fallen snow in our path. It was as if we had taken a covenant of silence, for I don't ever recall crying in her presence. Those morning walks we took became stories in themselves. I could distinguish between each one by something that had occurred, no matter how slight. The mist-ladened morning a cardinal signaled the close of winter by reappearing at different junctures in our stroll. First, in the tall hemlock, its branches burdened with drifting snow. Then on the gnarled black and budless limb of the apple tree that would soon come to life. Returning to my room that morning, we watched it ascend high above the woods before vanishing.

As she replaced me in the crib, I recall how dripping wet the hem of the scarlet-red scapular had become from brushing the snow path. When she gently shut the pine door, on the gray linoleum still lay the wet shadow of her presence.

Not unlike the trail of her cold fingers tracing the contours of my face, yet another daybreak.

Then I began to see her as my deaf-mute seasonal mother.

The garnet rosary beads . . . how they transfigured the morning light of my bedroom window. It became a secret the two of us shared those very early years.

Billy Coombs never knew.

* * *

But there was also present a sardonic humor, the existential kind.

How could Billy Coombs ever have seduced a nun? Particularly a paramour who eschewed self-discovery. He lived to entertain parasites . . . those who fed off his banal wisdom. The common man apotheosis. One who ceaselessly mocked what he knew but never admitted what was chasing him.

Even as a child I envisioned Billy Coombs running up neighborhood back alleys laughing uproariously. The residents in the surrounding houses likened the occasions to his conversations with God, which always occurred at nightfall.

Someone in each burg was assigned to do it. How Billy Coombs was appointed and by whom, no one knew. Or dared to ask for fear they might be appointed.

So, it was how I learned that Bernadette succumbed in childbirth . . . mine. In a burg such as ours, Ichabod and God were bedfellows. Just as Billy racing up backyard alleyways in semidarkness wasn't an anomaly.

One had to learn to pray like a deaf-mute if he or she wanted answers.

Grief, or the subliminal fear of it, was always real. That is why at night one could always hear the haunted words of the deceased emanating from the abandoned dam hollow at the end of County Line Road. Ossified with fear that someone we once knew intimately was calling out to us. Their summons congealed the heart.

Why Ichabod never smiled and hardly exchanged words with anyone; why bedridden Billy's mother longing to-meet-Jesus tore the scrim off my childhood dream; why the entire population of Berea deigned to lie that there was a valley of death.

While knowing full well that no one died. Ever.

Even Christ. For Billy told me so.

* * *

What else had he kept from me?

Those women who occasionally slept over a night or two in that early period of my life . . . how I had studied their miens to find some resemblance to mine. And only now to discover that the woman who bore me to life had committed hers to God. I'm hesitant to admit that it broke me up. In the privacy of my now unlocked domain, I laughed out loud. For Billy Coombs in my early years only slept with roundheels.

Independent of my naive grasp of procreation and the fuel that propelled two bodies together . . . I endeavored to envision Billy Coombs lifting the scarlet-red scapular off Bernadette's porcelain-white body.

The few times I approached the task late in the night when boyhood titillation may have produced an image in my head, the mind turned black. Followed immediately by my feeling deathly ill. Chastised. *But by whom?* I wondered. The parish priests? Ichabod, the son of Jesus? Franz, the Monsignor? The keening voices of the dead out County Line Road?

For committing sacrilege against the memory of my habit-swathed mother who had gone astray?

Except in her instance, thankfully, she was now real to me. Learning of her existence was my corporeal birthing experience. Knowing that she was once alive gave me life outside of my mind. I felt redeemed knowing that she lay alongside Billy Coombs to give me life.

For we exist in irony I realized.

Berea, the garden of my youth.

CHAPTER TWO

Now September, and the potted lily plant that Billy had gifted her that Easter Sunday sat dead outside her apartment door. Clumps of soil around its base suggested my grandfather had tripped over it several times when he returned long after midnight.

With the yolk-shaded sunlight bleeding from her parchment window blind, she spoke to me in a trance-like monotone about her and him.

"He arrived in this country, Jeremiah, the age you are today. With his two brothers from Germany."

She laughed, eyeing me to see if I caught the humor.

"I'm an Irish lass, you know. The potato famine swept my family across the Atlantic. We settled with my father's distant cousin in Erie, Pennsylvania. Attended school there along with my sister Bridget."

By then I knew her name was Agnes and my grandfather's, Jakob.

Seems he grew up in Toledo, Ohio, which also bordered Lake Erie. And at the age of sixteen began to frequent saloons. One evening after midnight, Jakob was drugged and shanghaied to serve on a tramp Lake Erie steamer for more than three years before he was released.

"Always carefree, your grandfather, Jeremiah. Even when he wasn't drinking Satan's Lager."

"How did you meet him?"

"It was the man's happy feet. Jakob was a natural-born dancer

. . . a tap dancer actually. Another abducted seaman who had been touring the towns surrounding the Great Lakes with their dancing troupe taught him how.

"Remember the silver tennis cups won by Franz I showed you? Well, open that top dresser drawer and you will see your grandfather's black leather tap shoes. You know, signs of sweeter days . . . or now, kinder hours before we say goodnight."

The votive light of her magnified liquid blue irises was flickering more erratically now, threatening to extinguish.

I muttered, "Happy feet?"

"My sister was two years older than me. There was this huge dance pavilion that extended out over Lake Erie. Where the best bands attracted hundreds of couples and loners like me and her summer weekend evenings. Jakob Coombs appeared out of the crowd and picked me instead of Bridget to dance.

"For me it felt like I was being elevated out of County Monaghan, Ireland, where . . .

> *My father played the melodeon,*
> *My mother milked the cows*
> *And I had a prayer like a white rose pinned*
> *On the Virgin Mary's blouse."*[2]

Agnes Coombs shut her eyes. The tortured fingers that tendrilled mine loosened their grip. I lifted the top hem of the faded patchwork quilt to cover her shoulders. Momentarily, I had the urge to lie alongside her but feared that Grandfather, once he returned home, might dance me about her bed.

* * *

A month later when I returned home from school I found him sitting alongside the console radio where he listened to the evening

---

2 Patrick Kavanagh: "My Father Played the Melodeon"

news. Except its red *on* light was dark, and he was doing something I had never once seen him do before.

"Why are you crying?"

He wouldn't answer.

I sat across from in a chair, waiting. Then I saw the garnet beads of his mother's rosary. Billy was rolling them between his thumb and index finger impulsively. I'd witnessed her caressing it during my visits.

"She's dead, isn't she?" I keened. *"She's fucking dead!"*

I blindly left the room and sat on the back stoop, crying louder than Billy Coombs. That perished Easter plant was the truth . . . bent over like her in that forsaken bed waiting for Jakob to bring home Christ so she could leave.

I ran back into the room.

"Finally you let me know there was somebody else in our family . . . other than just me and Billy Coombs. For all those boy years she lay alone down in that airless hovel, kept alive by muttering *Hail Mary's* echoing back to her like the ticking of a mantel clock.

"Didn't you imagine that I might take to somebody beside *you*, my fucking father?

"Maybe you don't think that way.

"No, of course you don't. My mother's name. She uttered it. Not you. Christ, you had me believing it was one of your whores. Well, Bernadette was the Christ whore . . . who lay with you. And do you think for one goddamn moment I'd love her any less? *Jesus God, Billy Coombs, I came out of her belly.* Doesn't that mean something to you? All those nights when I lay in bed as a dumb kid, crying for a mother I didn't have, and now yours is dead.

"Oh, Christ, yes. It all makes sense, doesn't it?

"Bawl you bastard, fucking bawl!"

I left the house that evening and didn't return for three days. I wandered aimlessly around Berea. When I was tired, I slept in an alleyway.

The late afternoon I returned home he eyed me sheepishly.

"I don't love those women I sleep with.

"But now you know the one I did. May your dreams be less troubled, Son.

"Go upstairs and get dressed. You'll get to meet my father and the Monsignor."

The wake was held in my uncle's parish house. Her casket was closed with a white lace chasuble draped across. Lit candle lobbers stood on either end and a single planted palm accompanied the kneeling stool in front of the bier.

I improvised the signs of the cross as I had not been baptized in the Roman Catholic faith. But I'd witnessed friends and neighbors do it often subconsciously alone. I also knelt and envisioned her eyeing me through the walnut coffer with her microscopic eyeglasses.

"Goodbye, sweet mother. You touched me like one. Until you, I always wondered how it felt."

Sitting in a separate room with Billy Coombs were two men. One very old with a high forehead topped by what appeared as a raven wig parted down the middle. It looked pasted on his pate. His skin was mottled and tanned as if he spent much time outside. And he grinned in a manner Ichabod never permitted himself to. Jakob Coombs was dressed in a white shirt buttoned at the neck with no tie, a black serge vest and black trousers which draped his shoes. I was unable to detect if they had tapping cleats.

"This is my father, Jeremiah. And alongside him, Monsignor Franz."

The contrast between the pair couldn't have been more pronounced.

Jakob looked like he could have been a circus performer. He radiated a human fun house whose doors led to nowhere, mirrors that prevaricated life, beefy calloused hands resting on his soiled pant legs aching to twirl you about the bier. One could never guess his lifelong mate lay stiff in the adjoining room.

And then there was Franz. His mother believed it was *he* who would save the family. The monsignor looked exactly like a saint on the RC annual calendar, marking one of its holy dates. He was tall, had a high neck, lips thinner than a persimmon and pale, virtually no hair except what sprouted out his nose, and huge ears that clung to his oval head like wet oak leaves.

When he spoke, he clipped his words implying he didn't exactly enjoy sharing them with me and Billy.

Franz kept telling Jakob how he was going to take him fly fishing. I could hardly suppress my laughter. *If you want to assuage the old man's grief,* I thought, *take him to a cat house.*

Fly fishing, for Chrissake! Why not teach him the Beatitudes in Greek?

The old man kept nodding his head with that incorruptible grin as he listened to his eldest son talk to him like a stranger.

My grandfather mindlessly listening to Franz palaver away while in the shadows of his consciousness he was thinking about returning to the empty bed that evening. The warm body alongside vanished.

The one lying wintry in the adjoining room with a *white rose pinned on the Virgin Mary's blouse.*

Billy gestured that we leave. Jakob interrupted Franz and reached out to grab my hand. "Mother spoke about you before she left."

Then he looked at my father.

"Bring him with you along next time. We'll go fishing." His toothless grin kindling the parish house.

And Christ's eyes over its hearth.

* * *

A Saturday morning that fall, Jakob Coombs knocked on our back door. Billy had left for the day. I asked Grandfather in but he shook his head and said our aged apple tree needed pruning. Attached to his belt like a scabbard dangled a large handsaw. He mentioned his son would surely agree, and began to climb the tree.

Periodically I'd peer out the kitchen window and watch large branches fall to the ground. At noon time, he climbed down and ambled off to the saloon at the end of our street. When I went out to inspect his labor, I became worried what Billy would say.

Jakob, it appeared, had confused pruning with mortally wounding. I feared that our harbinger of spring, Bernadette's and mine, would now die. Upon his return, Jakob, now under the weather, climbed to the top of what remained of the apple tree and sat there drunkenly gesticulating to the sky . . . like he was railing at someone or something.

A bird of Germanic origin cawing *Kaputtgebroche*[3] unrestrainedly.

I ran outside and begged him to come down.

Like he wasn't certain who or what he was.

"What do you want?" he burst.

"For you to come down out of our apple tree," or *What's left of it*, I thought.

"I'm not finished." He waved the handsaw at me menacingly.

Once again he resumed cutting off an additional branch . . . one to which Billy Coombs had attached an end of the clothesline that commenced from the corner of our house.

But the old man had tired himself out. Said he had to visit the monsignor for there was additional work there he had to finish before dark.

I helped him out of the tree. He hung one arm around my shoulder and motioned that we both step back to get a better vantage point to examine his work.

"*Es sieht gut aus, oder?*"[4]

I nodded.

"*Billy wird glücklich sein, nein?*"[5]

Jakob fumbled threading his belt through the saw handle. Then he wrapped his arms around me and once again muttered, "She liked you very much.

"Her Irish red hair. Like a fiery bird nesting up in that tree."

He was trying to tell me something.

---

3 Broken Broken

4 It looks good, right?

5 Billy will be happy, no?

"They fly off, you know?"

Wavering down our driveway, he turned, hollering back:

"My tap shoes. I'll let you try 'em on."

His laughter echoed over the backyard.

"She was always ready to dance, boy."

I never saw him alive again.

Billy Coombs returned home before dark. At first he didn't notice . . . until he poured himself a drink and stared dumbly out the back door's window.

The apple tree looked as if it had been denuded by an angry windstorm. Its branches pell-mell across the backyard like arms randomly ripped from its torso.

"Jakob dropped by this morning with his handsaw," I muttered.

"To Christ Almighty do what?"

"To prune. Claimed it would yield a bushel of Macs next year."

"What was he drinking? Fermented cider?"

He went outside and began angrily tossing the branches down over our backyard's hill that dropped steeply down to a creek that ran off from the limestone quarry at the top of our street.

Upon returning inside, he dropped spent into a kitchen chair.

"Now maybe you know why I stayed away all those years. The fucking tree is dead."

Billy's friend sawed it to but a foot off the ground the following spring.

* * *

Senescence rose like an oppressive bloom off the bodies of Jakob and Agnes Coombs. For him, it was the gamey nose of urine, perhaps days of it that had permanently impregnated his black serge trousers. She, on the other hand, emitted a stifling sweet odor, not unlike an Irish raisin bread pudding with cream lying forgotten in the afternoon sun.

Their distinctive personalities could not be ripped away from their mortal bouquets.

When Jakob stripped life from our apple tree that day, as he stood alongside, his foul odor caused me to imagine that he'd held a rotting condor he'd retrieved from a weathered nest high up in the branches in his beefy hands. Its parasitic insects and gut-roiling putrefaction caused me to turn my head away in repulsion.

His madcap grin not withstanding.

My father's blood standing before me . . . like the creek in our backyard rippling down from the limestone quarry at the top of our street.

And she, sweet Agnes, gifting me communion wafers laced with cinnamon for a long bus ride home.

The bells that tolled for each of them from the spire of Monsignor Franz's church in Sewickley rang clear and without dissonance.

Earth does not bury the rankness of time.

* * *

There were two hospitals in Berea. The Roman Catholic one, and the less prestigious one that was located in the southside of town populated mainly by immigrant families who worked in the nearby tin and bronze mills.

I followed my father inside the latter.

I recall its monastic interior with high ceilings feeling dark and tomb-like. Billy gestured to a wooden bench where I was to wait for him. While sitting there, I watched two orderlies wheel an occupied gurney out of the elevator to rumble over the polished floor tiles, echoing into the darkness. He returned, sat mutely alongside me, placed his hat on his knees, and stared straight ahead.

Conditioned to not ask questions until the passage of time revealed the answers, I envisioned Jakob appearing before Billy and me in a kaleidoscopic montage of circumstances. The rotting condor image was the most striking. He was dressed in surgical whites and was handing the defunct bird to my father as if he, Jakob, was the performing obstetrician. I began laughing to myself, only to be chastised by a swift elbow to my ribs.

Billy's eyes still fixed on a closed paneled door across from us.

When an unsettling moaning began to echo in the stone cavity of where we sat, intermittently pierced by a long, loud, high-pitched cry of pain emanating from behind that door.

"Ich kann es nicht mehr austehen!"[6]

Yet, those conducting the procedure didn't stop.

Soon it felt as if his cry was fading . . .

That the builder of bridges over Berea's twelve rivers, the German steeplejack who painted the gold crosses adorning Berea's parish roofs . . .

Wouldn't be dancing this night after work.

Until it became sepulchral quiet. The door that we watched never opened.

No sound of a gurney being wheeled to Christ knows where.

---

6 "I can't stand it any longer!"

Without a word between us in the car, we each climbed the stairs to our separate bedrooms.

At daybreak he drove off to work as I walked to school.

One night long after that day when Billy Coombs was deep in his cups, I broached the incident that he and I had silently witnessed.

"No anesthesia," he uttered.

And gestured to his heart as if it were Jakob's.

"What was wrong with him?"

"He couldn't piss."

* * *

Growing up in Berea, it was the rare occasion that I witnessed any male gesture to their brains in an effort to prove a point or punctuate something they passionately held to be the truth. Mostly it was to their genitals. Accompanied by a bawled, "Here!"

Which invariably settled the matter.

Ironically the locus was also our most vulnerable, be it from physical blow or a more existential assault, say, from a woman's rebuff.

My status among boyhood friends depended upon how well I lied about having sex. One quickly learned that rite of initiation: gesture to the triangle and holler, "Here. Eat this!"

It's why I found it so easy to yell "Fuck you!" to Billy Coombs when he was lugubrious over the death of his mother.

And when Billy answered *sotto voce*, "He couldn't piss," I surmised the surgeon was threading a scalpel up the dying man's urethra and not into his aorta valve. The utter expression of terror and agony mirroring Jakob's cries on my father's mien confirmed it.

Early on I was schooled in the disconnect between men like Billy Coombs who defined themselves by their sexual conquests while intimating it was the wooden cross each of them could perish on. Jakob Coombs, dancer and womanizer, was being taken out on Golgotha Hill's gurney of defunct pricks.

Conscience, hell! I'd think to myself when hearing one of St.

Andrew's nuns caution me to hear my conscience. "Who do you think is speaking to you?" they would point first to their heart then to mine. "It is none other than the Son of God."

But there was always a louder and more strident voice I heard as a boy. It was the same one our fathers listened to lying in bed next to our mothers . . . or women of pleasure.

Come daybreak we could all genuflect.

Several weeks following Jakob's passing, I knew Father had made peace with it. One Friday evening, long after I'd gone to bed, I awoke with a start, concerned that I hadn't heard him come home. Grandfather's demise curiously heightened my attachment to Billy. Prior, I would have rolled over and gone back to sleep. Instead I crossed our narrow upstairs hallway and opened the door to his room. The jaundice glow from the streetlight right outside our house illuminated his nude body and that of the woman who owned the bakery at the bottom of our street. Each dead to the world. On the floor at his side of the mattress in a pile lay his shirt, pants, and striped briefs.

Alongside, neatly paired together, Jakob's worn black patent-leather tap shoes.

Had he Bojangled the pruner's curse away that midnight up the carpeted stairs?

I could picture the two of them, stifling their laughter as a prelude to coitus. Billy stripped down, sans the old German's taps, and mounting the buxom confectioner.

With the iron bed springs accompaniment, the couple commenced warbling what was affectionally known in our town as the *Berea Canticle.*

CHAPTER THREE

Shortly following Jakob's death, was it a coincidence that Ichabod stopped in front of our house one evening upon returning home from work and wanly gestured *"Hello"* to me?

Billy ascended our front porch steps like it never happened.

Soon Ernest invited me to his bungalow, spartanly furnished, not unlike a country parish house. He offered me a glass of milk on a wooden tray. We sat there uncomfortably staring at each other. Finally, I said I had to go home. "I understand," he replied.

Those visits repeated themselves for several months. I felt I couldn't refuse when every couple of weeks on his way home from work—always with a nod of the head or left arm that was out of Billy's view—he'd extend the invitation.

That Christmas day when we sat down, he jumped up like he could wait no longer, disappeared down his cellar, only to return with a gift wrapped in butcher paper. While standing alongside nervously, he gestured that I open it.

It was a leather-covered writing journal. I looked up at him quizzically.

On the first page, unlined, were the handwritten words:

LESSON ONE

Followed by nothing else. The other unlined pages remained blank.

I closed the cover uncertain what to say.

It was at that moment Ichabod addressed me in a manner of a stranger living inside the person I'd learned to like.

"Jeremiah, from this moment on nothing will ever be the same between us. It mustn't frighten you, please. I detect anxiety creeping up your face.

"No, there is nothing to be afraid of. Trust me.

"Only wonderful occasions lie before us.

"This Sunday following Mass at St. Andrews, I want you to follow me home with your new ledger. I caution you to keep our visits and what occurs in them between us. Soon Billy Coombs will inquire what's going on. Just say we pass the time playing chess. That we enjoy each other's company. That's all.

"In time you will come to understand why I caution you so."

Ichabod bowed rigidly to me and disappeared into the kitchen.

* * *

That Sabbath he took me on a brief tour of his bungalow. Upstairs across from his monastic bedroom, he showed me a room with shelves of material for sewing costumes, mannequin body forms for fitting, sewing machines.

A miniature theater he'd set up in his basement. The stage platform was outfitted with a velvet curtain that opened and closed by ropes and pulleys. Chairs lined up in front of it in rows. There were also stage lights rigged up to a sound board behind the seating.

This is where, for the next couple of years our friendship occurred. It is where I was instructed by him, through theater . . . words and plays, performances . . . as to what he had learned and observed about life through extensive reading from Catholic sources and the travels he'd made prior to settling on our street.

As to why he settled in Berea, judging by his guarded allusions over time, I sensed it was because of some intimate relationship with a member or members of my family. A story that would ultimately be revealed.

But first it was mostly a teaching experience for me. "You will learn from various playwrights, Jeremiah. Aeschylus, an ancient

Greek author who is often described as the father of tragedy. Bertolt Brecht. Eugene Ionesco. Samuel Beckett, perhaps. The performances will be memorable but short."

He promised stories from various authors dramatized in a similar manner, while enunciating their names like they were beloved family members: Franz Kafka, Ivan Turgenev, Isaac Babel, Sherwood Anderson, Washington Irving, Flannery O'Connor.

Ichabod became these characters.

* * *

I sat in the first row.

In my lap rested the journal he had gifted me . . . its pages still blank.

There were muffled sounds coming from behind the dark blue curtain. A spotlight fell on its cleavage. Ernest appeared, took a slight bow, and proclaimed:

"This afternoon I am going to tell you a story about some of the people you know, about what we have experienced with rationed food and gasoline, safety air raid blackouts, the deafening sirens, the dark Führer movies . . ." Ichabod visibly shuddered. "The dread that has creeped into our bones like a disease."

I could only concur. Even Billy Coombs's upbeat attitude appeared to be weighed down by the war in Germany. For he could be called up any day. We made an effort not to discuss it at dinner.

Ichabod began reading:

Chester Grange Joined the Marines.

He left his harmonicas at home. Mrs. Grange displayed the prized collection on the fireplace mantel under her son's portrait. When Mother and I would visit, she'd place one of the instruments in my hand. "Please don't try to play it, Jimmy. Chester's breath is still inside its reeds. Mustn't let it escape till he returns from parachuting behind enemy lines. Then I'll bet he'll let you have one of 'em." The women stayed close by, eyeing me periodically while they conversed to make certain I didn't put the harp to my lips.

A service flag with one blue star graced her living room window. Several gold stars hung in the neighbors' windows.

But then the stage lights kept flickering on and off accompanied by the ubiquitous Berea air raid sirens. Ichabod kept reading, except I couldn't hear him. The story had fractured like a movie projector's sprocketing . . . until normalcy resumed.

. . . when we'd sit in the airless living room on overstuffed furniture decorated with crocheted antimacassars, I imagined Chester had already come home. Not in his Marine blues, mind you. But his ghost. For when the women leaned close to each other, shaking their heads, often grievously, about the murderous Krauts and all the terrible things that were occurring in the Pacific, I imagined Chester was holding off until he could find the courage to say—"I'm dead."

"You sure Chester is still alive, Ma?" I inquired the day she drove the back roads home.

"Why do you ask?"

"'Cause it feels like we're visiting the undertaker's when we go there. The harmonicas clutching his breath—plus that painting of him in his uniform holding rosary beads."

"Chester's still writing to his mother, Jimmy. How could he be deceased?"

But soon the letters stopped. It was as if Mrs. Grange had expected as much for she quit waiting for the postman. Once we heard his footsteps on her porch. "Oh, Beatrice," Mother exclaimed, "maybe they'll be some word from Chester."

Her friend smiled transcendently and shook her head. "No," she said . . .

Again scripted pandemonium aborted Ichabod's theater. Lights off and on, war engines whose klaxons awoke even the dead.

" . . . my boy who'd awake me in the middle of the night, naked as a blue jay, trembling. 'What is it, Chester?' I'd ask. 'What's wrong?' He'd reply, 'I don't want the Gestapo to take you away, Mama.' I'd laugh, Rose. But the dear shivered like he'd caught a chill. Then I said, 'You're afraid of dying, aren't you, Son?' That's when he wept."

She handed the harmonica to my mother who took a deep whiff of the air holes—lingered—then handed it back.

"What's it smell like to you, Rose?"

"Tree bark," Mother said.

Mrs. Grange nodded as if she had been told the God's truth. She promptly bundled all the harmonicas into the center of her dress, lifted its hem to form a basket, waddled over to the mantle, and returned them to their rightful place—except one.

The chromatic one, long as a schoolhouse ruler, she handed to me.

"Blow in it, Jimmy. Chester's dead."

The entire cellar went black. The only sound was that of Ichabod's labored breathing. His occasional words punctuated what felt like the stopping of time. A neighborhood dog's barking restored my host's fragmented reading.

". . . week I took my Hohner Chromonica to school.

"A Marine who's fighting the Krauts gave me his prize harmonica, Mrs. Gresham. I'd like to perform for the class."

She shot me a dubious glance. "You know how to play the harmonica?"

"Yes ma'am, I do. Lieutenant Chester Grange, OSS, taught me how."

I held it to my mouth and pressed the silver plunger several times to give her the impression that I knew exactly what I was doing.

"Are you sure, Jimmy?"

"Scout's honor," I replied.

The rhythm band had already assembled before the blackboard.

"Jimmy Rogues is going to serenade us today, class," she announced.

I stood before my friend Jack Murphy who played the sand blocks.

When I exhibited the prodigious instrument, several classmates stared at me incredulously. A few tittered.

"What tune are you going to play for us, Jimmy?" Mrs. Gresham asked.

"Night Rain," I said. "It's my very own composition."

I'd been blowing and drawing on the air holes all week long, and I would demonstrate the entire range of the harp's *orkestra's* effects. One I'd really worked on was sliding it back and forth between my lips like I was wetting a jumbo cigarette paper—but rapidly while pumping the octave plunger mercilessly.

It would lift them out of their seats.

I started out *adagio*, creating a long low train whistle. They could appreciate that. Then as the locomotive gained on us—*allegretto, allegro*—I began jumping octaves.

Soon, I was so into blowing and sucking all the wind I could muster that the classmates began snorting. Mrs. Gresham cracked her heels against the hardwood floor in an effort to shush them. Jack Murphy had begun playing the sand blocks behind his head; the castanet duo mocked Lone Ranger and Tonto's horses slowing to a trot; Betsy Tinsley struck the silver "attention, class" bell on Mrs. Gresham's desk with her triangle mallet; and the tambourine trio feigned gagging while whacking the instruments on the heads of the rhythm stick Calucca twins.

By now, I was wheezing and sucking *prestissimo* and my face had turned beet-red as I approached the apogee of "Night Rain"—when Mrs. Gresham peremptorily yanked the chromatic out of my mouth and snapped that I sit down.

The band dropped their instruments into the large chest and quickly slid into their seats.

I began to cry.

"Well," she spat, "you said you knew how to play the . . . MOUTH ORGAN."

"I do," I said.

"What was that we just heard?"

My classmates clasped their hands over their mouths.

"A symphony for Chester Grange—*a dead Marine.*"

"Oh." She took a deep breath, a blush creeping up her neck. "Yes— well, give James a nice hand, class." While the students politely applauded, Murphy put his fingers to his lips and made an earsplitting whistle.

Ichabod withdrew from inside his jacket a sterling silver Chromonica, placed it to his lips, and began to perform "Butterfield's Lullaby," the twenty-four-note final bugle call. Yet no sound emerged from his instrument.

"But wait," I said, "I'm not finished."

Before she could object I began playing *Taps*. That I'd truly mastered in my bedroom over the days. I'd made it sound like a coronet. All single notes and just as mournful. It was really Chester's breath, not mine. He was playing at his own graveside, breathing his own requiem.

Now the classmates sat soberly. All wide-eyed and beginning to look forlorn, for most had a brother, father, uncle, or close family friend who had perished in the war. It had touched every street in our town it seemed. Gold stars on white flags were multiplying outside drawn Venetian blinds or opaque green shades.

Once, poster cards hung in some of the windows, informing the iceman how much to drop off that day—a twenty-five-pound or fifty-pound block. Now, stars of the dead.

And the mute basketball court behind our school where many of the young warriors once congregated at dusk had swallowed their raucous laughter. But in this moment I imagined the dead souls rising out of the cracked macadam with Marine Band harps to begin singing final breaths they'd rationed for their loved ones—and the skirts who appeared after dark to burnish the nickel-plated night its chill—echoing Chester's requiem.

The haunting cry of *Taps* reverberated down the school building's terrazzo hallways. I could hear classroom doors opening for now Chester was bitterly inspired, and he played a second chorus even more plaintive than the first.

I watched Mrs. Gresham sink into her desk chair and drop her head into her hands. The children laid their heads onto their desks, too, and some began to weep.

And I felt ashamed holding Chester's harmonica while he was performing. I felt like a paper soldier. For I'd done nothing except smell his breath.

And pretend I was a musician. While he was the star.

Ichabod disappeared behind the curtain. I sat there in a charged emotional state. Everyone on our street knew Chester had recently perished in the war. One couldn't help but hurry to their windows and witness Mrs. Grange walk past, returning from the corner grocery store.

Words, especially too many of them, become tedious.

Yet, my new friend's reading had moved me nearly to tears.

Billy Coombs could rarely do that.

Ichabod spoke up from behind the curtain.

"Lesson One!" he reiterated like he'd just closed a large tome. "Dead harmonica player will accompany you home."

By now it had turned dusk outside.

Caught up in what had transpired in Ernest's house, I hadn't noticed that indeed it felt like a person was walking alongside me. He was gazing about like he'd just returned to a place fondly remembered. Even pointed to a house where young Eva Butter once lived. I smiled like he and she were both alive.

Once inside my place, he followed me around deferentially.

At first it made me uncomfortable.

Feeling the urge to shake it off, I splashed cold water on my face and stared into the medicine cabinet mirror to satisfy myself Chester Grange wasn't standing behind me.

Billy still hadn't returned by 10:00 p.m. I'd given my word to keep mum about all that did occur and would happen over the months ahead with Ichabod Tyner. I felt, nonetheless, a return to some day-to-day reality might be a tonic.

It was in bed, however, that I knew something had changed forever.

Chester lay asleep. Happy to be home.

Initially, I was loath to crawl in alongside him for fear he would smell of death. But he emitted the cool odor of rusty orange creek mud that formed the bed of the limestone quarry runoff from the top of our street as it coursed through backyards on its path to one of Berea's twelve rivers. Having dammed our creek as a boy, the mud felt soft like skin, its texture saturated. I rolled it between my hands to form clay walls alongside its path.

Only the creek made rippling noises as it passed through.

Lying there I couldn't even hear Chester breathe.

* * *

By chance the next morning I passed Mrs. Grange in an aisle of the local grocery store and froze. *Christ, she will see Chester!*

"Good morning, Jeremiah. I'm surprised to see you here so early."

"Low on milk and cereal," I replied meekly.

She moved on past me as if it were yesterday when the sky was cerulean blue with no rain cloud in sight. I couldn't help but anguishing Chester would somehow signal her.

But he didn't stir.

And as I walked back to our house, I began to understand that Billy Coombs and I were no longer alone. There was a harmonica player who shared my bedroom, except Billy would never hear or speak to him. Just like my deceased mother looked after me in my infant years. I saw her, but no one else attested to her presence.

As they wouldn't Chester's either.

Even though he shared my nightly bed. Walked alongside me to school each weekday morning. Listened to my stories. Smirked when I lied to him.

Happiest when we'd stroll by Eva Butter's house.

My brother who couldn't speak.

And no one knew. Except Ichabod . . . maybe.

CHAPTER FOUR

A whole week had passed before Ernest acknowledged my presence again as he exited St. Andrews Mass that Sunday. "This afternoon at 4:00. Bring Chester." Despite my having no choice but to arrive accompanied, he hollered from upstairs to head down to his theater. When he appeared, looking a shade forlorn, Ichabod placed a wooden chair in the center of the stage and sat down, eyeing me the entire time.

"Are you and Chester getting along?"

"Oh, yes."

"Good." He nodded but still preoccupied.

"I didn't intend for it to happen so rapidly, Jeremiah."

"I'm not understanding."

"Chester's mother couldn't have withstood his showing up at her front door."

"Oh, we're fine," I enthused. "I walk him by Eva Butter's old place nightly."

Ichabod actually laughed. More of a guttural chuckle actually. "Have you begun to figure out why we are doing this, son?" He caught me unaware. "I mean our visits and my relationship to your father. It is all a mystery to you still, no?"

"It has always felt that way with Billy."

"I've known him for a very long time."

"My mother, too?"

Ichabod shook his head. "I can't tell you more now."

"Why?"

"What I can say is that she never wandered back from County Line Road. Those who have did so because they longed to return home. Except she didn't have one."

Once again the room became pitch black. Within seconds the familiar air raid warning sirens began screaming, only to fade out before they rose to an unbearable pitch again. What followed sounded as if it were coming from a ham radio. In fact I was almost certain I could envision a shadowy figure bending close to a faintly illuminated red dial as Ichabod impersonated my wartime forebodings.

> Upon hearing Mrs. Paczynski's tell of *Der weisse Engle*[7] at the train platform, the man became for me the uber face of evil. He was the GOD we could see—the evil, sinister god.
>
> The SS Hauptstrumfuhrer[8] in a laboratory jacket now resided to the right of my bed, inches away from the north window that overlooked the backyard and the narrow creek that knifed through it on its way from the quarry to the dark Neshannock.

"Doesn't one of them ever want to crawl under the covers and strangle one of us?"

It was the Holy Ventriloquist again.

When the room turned ink black, he slipped out of bed and stood in one of the corners. I could see him because he had taken the glowing crucifix and hung it by a shoestring about his neck. The neon green cross dangling just above his heart.

"What are you doing?"

"Trying to make 'em go away for you. It's what our priests are able to do, you know. Scare the evil spirits away."

"Well, the Schutzstaffel[9] don't believe in the devil."

---

7 The white Angel

8 Hauptsturmführer—a Nazi Party paramilitary rank

9 SS committed war crimes and crimes against humanity during World War II (1939–45).

"*Schutzstaffel?*"

"Yeah. Furthermore, he ain't in that corner."

"Who ain't?"

"The White Angel."

"Who's he?"

"He kills kids who ain't twins, dwarfs, or hunchbacks."

My conscience crawled back into bed. The crucifix still on his bare chest.

"How?"

"Sending them with their parents to a big room with hundreds of others where the ceiling don't got rivers like ours but is lined with shower heads, the big watering-can kind like mamas use for roses. Except no water ever comes out of the little pinholes in the brass nozzles. Just *hissssssing.*"

"Hissing?"

The beams of a passing truck circled our room's walls like searchlights.

"So, Christman, go into that corner and give him a hug. He's got blue eyes and is all dressed up in his bespoke uniform. His boots, rising up to his knees, shine so that you can see your face in them. Get a good glimpse of your alabaster mug, 'cause he'll point his baton to the window. That means you're gonna drown and float down to the dark Neshannock, then out to the Ohio. The Neshannock is the river of death."

I could see *Onkel Mengele* as clear as I could picture our own Celestial Father standing there.

When the stage lights illuminated, the person sitting alongside a Bakelite radio turned facing Chester and me. It wasn't Onkel Mengele but Jakob Coombs. Our Steeplejack of the Cross . . . Bojangles of Death tap dancing about the neighborhood at night with the handsaw jiggling off his leather belt.

Onkel Jakob. Precursor of Zyclon B.

"Permit me to prune your apple tree, Lili Marlene."

Vor der Kaserne
Vor dem grossen Tor
Stand eine Laterne
Und steht sie noch davor
So woll'n wir uns da wieder seh'n
Bei der Laterne wollen wir steh'n
Wie einst Lili Marleen
Wie einst Lili Marleen[10]

All the while grinning broadly at me.

Air raid sirens whined again only this time they sounded much farther away.

---

10 *In front of the barracks* **Before** *the giant gate* **There** *stands a streetlamp* **It's** *where we used to wait* **And** *if that streetlamp still burns bright* **We'll** *stand again beneath its light* **Like** *back then Lili Marleen* **Like** *back then Lili Marleen*

The lights began to fade. With the stage once again bathed in darkness, I could barely make out Grandfather's person.

His silhouette illuminated by a distant votive candlelight.

I remained seated, awaiting instructions from Ernest. But none were uttered.

I walked back home. Passing each of the neighbor's houses, and envisioned Onkel Jakob watching me from their front porch or from behind Eva Butter's bedroom window.

Would he be awaiting me in our kitchen?

Or sharing Father's bed in Billy Coombs's absence?

Atop our porcelain-white Frigidaire the Bakelite radio was playing "Lily Marlene."

Onkel Jakob Bojangles, his wooden taps brushing each stair to my room like breath.

* * *

As I lay alongside Chester that Sunday night—each of us awake at daybreak—I was comforted by his presence, for I felt I was now witnessing:

LESSON TWO

Never called out by Ichabod, but why name truths that one could never forget?

Onkel Jakob lay on the other side of me this night. He lurked behind every door in our house. Not unlike a scalpel, his handsaw lay at our bedside. His labored breaths at times mocking Father's peccadillos with the local parish woman we knew as the Polish Accordion.

Our Lily Marlene. Our Mother of the Steeplejack Cross.

Our blood who wheezed gas.

Following my second Sunday visit to Ernest's house, I returned home from school that Friday afternoon to see Chester and Eva sitting next to each other on our living room sofa, waiting. Neither spoke but scowled at me accusingly.

The anguish of her expression triggered my flashback.

I recalled joining a pack of neighborhood boys at Berea's Municipal Park swimming pool three years earlier, surrounding Eva Butter underwater to wrest her bathing suit off her bony chest both in fun and a blind sexual urge. The incandescent rumor spread among us was that she had a gold star tattooed over her left nipple.

Eva escaped unclothed but was subsequently caught in the suction from an open culvert that flushed pool water down into the Neshannock River and drowned.

From that day forward there was always a pale yellow light left on in the upper floor of her house.

Eva's mother, Sophia, worked at the pottery mill, and for years the men on our street would ogle her stepping off the bus at dinner time and walking up the macadam to her house. She had brown curly hair and was an adult version of lovely young Eva who exhibited a flirtatious air. One got the impression in observing either mother or daughter that each delighted in their identity as sensuous women, neither chary to ginger up the neighborhood where too often the nuns and widows garmented in black muffling paraded its sidewalks.

Sophia's evening perambulation from work had become St. Andrew's tonic to its male parishioners.

But coincident with the start of Berea's biweekly air raid siren exercises, whisperings about Sophia Butter began to take hold in the parish. For several years when the family had moved up our street, only the men took notice of the Mrs.

With the advent of *Kristallnacht*, I began hearing women customers at the local bakery speaking in dampened voices about the "Jewess of Cascade Street." Now they, too, began to watch her step off the bus after work. Often gathered in pairs like glistening ravens.

Sophia opted to wear a heavy overcoat before the street's aged oak trees shed their leaves. She tied her hair in a tight bun and covered it with a dun-shaded scarf.

Music expired from her stride.

Then Eva drowned.

And now the Sophia Butter's pale yellow light remained constant even during the air raid klaxons when all the other houses on our street had turned black.

It was in those deafening moments that Eva reappeared alongside Chester, clinging to each other in a corner of my bedroom while the blankets covering the windows scarcely veiled our impending doom.

Arousal and Thanatos.

The stain that's never erased on Billy Coombs's street.

* * *

The sirens had not ceased until two o'clock that morning.

Eva and Chester remained wide awake as did I. Eva began talking about going to school again. She started to catalog the clothes in her closet . . . which of course had stood empty for years. Chester longed for his Chromonica as if somehow it could miraculously allay the caw of fate the sirens had stirred within us.

It was only then we heard Billy's footsteps on the stairs joined by another pair, heading to his bedroom across the tiny hallway from ours . . .

Eva whispered, *"Magdalena."*

Yes, the bakery owner who made and sold creampuffs every Saturday morning. How could she not have become an integral part of our childhoods? It was a rare Saturday when its doors opened that several of us neighborhood kids weren't waiting in line with our silver nickels clenched tightly in our fists.

Then: *"Shhh. We mustn't awaken Jeremiah."*

No starlight cast over our bodies.

"Do they leave their door open?" Chester muttered.

Where earlier we were iced with fear . . . now each of us had swollen with lust like Magdalena's pastries.

Eva cupped her hands against her ears. *"She's begun . . . the Flour Sifter's begun to moan. Christ, can't you hear her?"*

Chester wanted to crawl across the hallway to see if he could witness.

"What if they catch you?" I said.

Eva and he audibly laughed. "What would they see, Jeremiah?"

The sounds of copulating began to billow. The bed springs' squeaking accompanied Billy Coombs' violent thrusts into Magdalena, provoking a *"Yes"* arpeggio. Again and again up her keyboard. *"Yes. Please Yes. Yes. Yes. And Yes."*

"Oh Christ!" Eva cried. "Come the Messerschmitts!"

Billy began to rasp libidinously to Magdalena. *"What I am going to do when I finish fucking you, Woman."* Then he referenced the creampuffs. It sounded like they were masticating the mattress.

Chester, Eva, and I simultaneously pictured her lying nude in the pastry case, covered in powdered sugar.

It was in that moment Eva tore the blanket off our bedroom window.

I can only attempt to describe what I saw in the minutes that followed. Not across the hall but in my very room, for the amber glow of the streetlight outside our house now flooded the bedroom's corner were she and Chester huddled close to each other when the sirens screamed across Berea's twelve rivers.

Sitting alongside Chester, she methodically sewed his eyelids shut.

The thread glittered like yellow silk with each stitch. He neither flinched nor winced. Then it was his turn. Three stitches each eye.

Noisy coitus occurring across the hall.

Seamstress and seamster now sat benumbed in their niche. Their windows dark.

I heard Magdalena descend the stairs before daybreak.

Soon the glacé bakery fumes would waft through St. Andrews's nave.

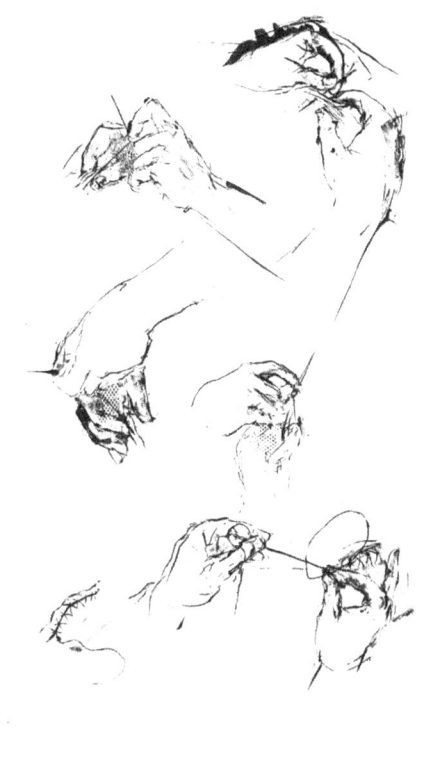

* * *

It was on the third night of their disappearance that first Eva, and then Chester, reappeared ... but in a dream fraught with foreboding. Returning from County Line Road, Onkel Jakob cradled Eva in his arms, with Chester shadowing them closely behind.

Her feet were bare and bore signs of abrasions as if she had walked a long distance prior to his carrying her. Nascent signs of bruising had begun to discolor the flesh surrounding her eyelid sutures. Onkel's scabbard handsaw at times scrapped the road's surface like a malignant counterpoint to the trio's midnight parade with Chester blowing *An die Freude* on his ten-hole pocket harmonica.

They stopped outside Ichabod's bungalow. Onkel Jakob bowed

deferentially to Ernest as if to acknowledge their longtime acquaintance.

We were invited into the house and followed our host down into the basement. Ichabod climbed onto the stage, passed his journal to Onkel Jakob, requesting he read from it. Instead, the old man ushered Chester behind the lectern, handed off the notebook to him, while he and Eva slid into the proscenium's darkness.

His eyelids still sutured shut, Chester read from Ichabod's story.

Since You Asked

Leopards break into the temple and drink the sacrificial chalices dry; this occurs repeatedly, again and again; finally it can be reckoned upon beforehand and becomes part of the ceremony.

—Franz Kafka

The evening I arrived in Prague, boots and women's hard leather heels clattering on the cobble lane outside my hotel window had arrested my sleep. From my youth I recalled black-and-white movies of the Geheime Staatspolizei[11] marching from house to house. Their pulse on the stones so profound to me I'd break out in a cold sweat.

Were they coming for my mother, Shulamit? And since my train to Prague had taken me through Czechoslovakia, I knew somewhere alongside its sparse countryside tracks Terezin once existed.

Crossing the Charles Bridge, its parapets aligned by the effigies of twenty-one Roman Catholic saints, I ascended the Little Quarter hill to Prague Castle and St. Vitus Cathedral, situated within the palace grounds. Directly outside the castle walls a series of small cottages had been constructed early on for its artisans. Seeking a quieter, more secluded place to write away from his Old Town apartment, Kafka, with his favorite sister Ottla, had rented one. Each afternoon, following his duties as officer for the Worker's Accident Insurance Company, he would tramp across the bridge

---

11 Secret State Police

and climb the steep path to Golden Lane. Late in the evening he'd retrace his steps back across the silvery Vltava River.

But it was on the Charles Bridge itself where he often lingered.

For there rose a solitary wooden crucifix that for two centuries stood alone on the span before the sandstone saints had appeared, and attached to its single crosspiece to which the sufferer's arms were nailed hung a swag of golden Hebrew letters: *Holy, Holy, Holy Lord*, endowed by a Jew as punishment for a blasphemy.

What occurred in the author's head each time he passed the gilded rood? I wondered. Did Kafka chant the words as if to forsake them, marking that a brethren had been forced to sing and pay for them? Perhaps he found them sardonically emblematic of *his* own daily rounds: *Holy, Holy, Holy Lord* parroted to the Czech shopkeepers, the sentry at the palace gates, the sexton at St. Vitus Cathedral, or the astronomical clock keeper steps from Franz's residence. How dissimilar was it from costuming himself in tailored livery while inhabiting the halls of bureaucracy, its airless chambers of papers and numbers, each day . . . before retiring to his room to write of penal colonies, hunger artists, or Gregor Samsa transmogrifying into a roach?

If queried about the embellished Crucifix, would Kafka have feigned anger and charged, "Whose profanity?" yet quickly add, "Gold for *Holy, Holy, Holy Lord*? The pious ones could have severed the offender's head and displayed it in the bridge's Old Town Tower as had occurred in the past to others less fortunate. Like poor John Nepomuk, they might have bound and pitched him to his death into the cruel Vltava."

For good luck, scores of the span's daily peripatetic rubbed a bronze relief depicting the latter incident, causing the trussed body of the saint to shimmer like a coin. *Surely Kafka witnessed that ritual.* And Saints Joseph, Ann, Francis Xavier, Christopher, Anthony, Jude, Augustine, plus the thirteen remaining the writer passed twice daily on the Charles Bridge—is it unreasonable to conjecture he greeted several by name, fancying that it was the token required of all Jew's who cross the Vltava? And for good measure caressed the coin of St. John Nepomuk, too?

On the pedestrian bridge, I was continually unnerved by heeltaps striking the cobblestones, erupting like paper caps, advancing toward me or approaching from behind. A person was inclined neither to look up nor over his shoulder.

Out of the shadows Franz K. stepped forward and cleared his throat:

"A parody. Every last day of my life. I had nobody to speak it to save for a few close friends. Late afternoons and evenings the script filled more notebooks. They piled up, collecting dust under my bed, on various surfaces in Old Town, and outside the castle walls on Golden Lane. I dressed each morning in proper attire and conducted myself in society as if there were nothing so grotesquely mad to laugh at. Often when I crossed the Charles Bridge, staring down at the silvery Vltava, I wished to dissolve myself and the history of my race into its icy swell.

"There was no succor.

"Except the farce, that is. Who I was and those about me under our garments, behind the velvet curtain. The theater in my belfry was what sustained me. The little plays that I would act in and entertain myself alone at night in my study.

"And the black joy, twice each day, muttering the words that the blasphemous Jew was ordered to purchase so that the naked Christ would have a swag of Hebraic letters adorn his torso. Did they beat the poor man? Did they make him recite Holy, Holy, Holy Lord until he was blue in the face? How much gold did they squeeze out of the fool? And, pray tell, what could he have uttered that so outraged the hierarchy?

"That we are guilty for being alive?

"The black absurdity of it all. I was Franz K., the roach, hunger artist, a lawyer for Worker's Accident Insurance Company.

"Until I heard the boots, that is, drumming the cobblestones behind me.

"Their echo against the granite markers in the Old Jewish Cemetery.

"Outside my deathbed, they stormed the sanatorium's marble hall-

way. But then I was without tongue. Only slips of paper could answer
for me . . .
  "Holy, Holy, Holy Lord, we sing."

The lights began to flicker amid what sounded like a battalion of troops marching up the street outside Ichabod Tyner's house.

Eva vaulted out of the shadows. "We must hide under the bed!" she cried.

"Bed?" Chester laughed. "But you stored it away with your wedding dress. Onkel has forgotten his toast to you and me. Just as well. It was in German . . . and the boots sing more eloquently than slurred words. Pour him another beer. Perhaps he will dance with the Crucifix on our wooden table. Onkel Jakob of the Cross. Bojangle of Christ."

My father played the melodeon,
My mother milked the cows
And I had a prayer like a white rose pinned
On the Virgin Mary's blouse.[12]

Onkel had climbed upon the table, warbling the familiar verse.

A white rose pinned to his black-garmented chest, he chants the *Hail Mary*:

Gegrüßet seist du, Maria, voll der Gnade,
der Herr ist mit dir.
Du bist gebenedeit unter den Frauen,
und gebenedeit ist die Frucht deines Leibes,
Jesus.
Heilige Maria, Mutter Gottes,
bitte für uns Sünder,
jetzt und in der Stunde unseres Todes. Amen.[13]

---

12 Patrick Kavanagh: "My Father Played the Melodeon"

13 Hail, Mary, full of grace, the Lord is with thee. Blessed art thou amongst women and blessed is the fruit of thy womb, Jesus. Holy Mary, Mother of God, pray for us sinners, now and at the hour of our death. Amen.

Joined by Chester, Eva stepped to the stage's apron.

"Jeremiah, we must leave now. It is time you author your story. Your bedroom's corner where he and I hunkered like children as the sirens whined . . . we bequeath those memories to you, dear friend.

"For death shows no mercy.

"Eva's nothing more than a desiccated sunflower. Chester, a mute ten-hole harmonica. And Christ, but a muddy creek in Berea.

"Jakob's blood runs cold in our veins.

"He won't entertain without an audience."

* * *

Briskly exiting the performance, I returned to our house alone, vainly calling out in the rooms to see if either Eva or Chester was there.

A rapping on the kitchen door's window startled me.

"I have something to tell you. It is about your mother."

Ichabod, looking like a refugee from the camp, wore a gold star pinned to his garment.

"Jeremiah. Your childhood is nearly over. Only the ghosts like myself and Onkel Jakob will keep you from forgetting. Tonight was the final performance in my basement's theater.

"It's all been for your benefit."

"But why?" I ask.

"Because she was not here to tell you herself."

"I don't understand."

"Let me explain what until now remained hidden from you."

We sit at the kitchen table.

"Bernadette—her preferred name—was my sister Hannah. We, like Eva's family, settled in Berea upon fleeing from Poland in the '30s. This neighborhood was very much as it exists today. Mostly Italians who emigrated to America. St. Andrews parish its spiritual heart.

"Of course our parents never became parishioners, but felt welcomed into the community. My father became a shoemaker.

When war was declared by the Germans and with news of the Polish Jews being rounded up, nearly overnight Hannah became possessed by God and joined the church. It was as if she began to view herself as one of the saints on St. Andrews annual calendar. She even began dressing like one, wearing a white cloth over her hair. I'd hear her fervent prayers each night at bedtime from an adjoining room. Our folks didn't know what to make of it.

"One day she announced she was leaving to join a priory. Hannah had just completed the eleventh grade, and that very night she began to pack her clothes.

"Mother was beside herself.

"We watched her get on the Greyhound bus the next morning. The Sisters of Conscience, a small convent in Ohio, had welcomed her. "I'll write once I get settled," she promised.

"Except there was something we didn't know.

"Billy Coombs had arrived before God.

"Hannah, together with her worldly belongings, was carrying *you* on the Greyhound.

"How the conception occurred, we never learned.

"Had it occurred one summer night along the creek bed? Surely it happened with other neighborhood girls her age. Except they didn't wear a white cloth over their head and pray for Christ to enter their hearts to cleanse them from sin. Nor did they weep at night alone in their beds for their relatives being rounded up like cattle for slaughter.

"Like her story, Jeremiah, we were never told its ending. It was the last I saw her that early morning."

"What do you think happened to her?"

Ichabod stared at me before muttering, "My guess?"

"Yes."

"She stepped off the bus at Portsmouth, Ohio, the confluence of the Ohio and Scioto Rivers. It's listed as your place of birth on the certificate. Mother was called several weeks following her absence. A note had been left with you in a tidy bundle on the convent steps.

"I believe Hannah continued on by foot to Cairo, Illinois where she and the Ohio joined the Mississippi."

"So, it's why you befriended Billy Coombs?"

"I felt I owed it to your mother and you."

"Onkel Jakob. Where does he come in?"

"He carries his own shadow . . . like each of us. Only his is darker."

Mother's pilgrimage I envisioned tailing the Ohio's swell through West Virginia and Kentucky, the southern borders of Ohio, Indiana, and Illinois until she joined the mighty Mississippi River at the city of Little Egypt. A white head scarf trailing in her wake.

. . . Aching to embrace Billy's trunk as he had Ichabod's, I watched the twosome spinning away from me and feared being swallowed by the armory's stygian gloom. That he and Ernest were another star gamboling off into the shadowy ceiling, and I was left to join the blank-face riders awaiting the Greyhound's summons. That one man clinging onto another for dear life was levitating away from the assembled dead, rising above Ohio Valley's Sunday graveyard . . . escaping its pull of ennui and malaise.

Nights I even fancy myself charging after the pair, but am dissuaded by the anesthetized passengers who barely raise their heads, the smokers their jaundiced eyes.

The kid will never catch up with the whirling duo, they mutter.

As if the homebound perceive that some men are dancers born to transcend darkness. To whirl about on the world's illusory stage.

That's just how it is.

Yeah, sure your old man loves you. Have another ham sandwich, kid. They're a bit stale by now. Here, put some catsup and relish on it. Do you want a soda?

Come back to the bus with us.

You won't tell your ma, will you?

That's Ernie "Ichabod" Tyner. He's a dipper like your old man at the pottery. Quite a stepper, too, don't you agree?

That's how we keep the light on, kid.

Can't take any of this life seriously.

Billy Coombs don't.

* * *

I had no intention of leaving Berea.

Yet I'd lived long enough not to take anybody at their word.

Take my grandfather, for instance. Everything I've said about him thus far is true. *Yet how can that be?*

He passed away soon after Victory in Europe Day. Billy Coombs took me to his wake. Dressed him in a three-piece suit purchased from Salvation Army. Monsignor had threaded a rosary in his father's cold hands. Billy insisted he be interred along with the tapping shoes.

Except that very night as Billy lay in his room, and I in mine a hallway's width away, each of us could plainly hear Jakob pacing downstairs, his handsaw scrapping across the hardwood floor.

Nobody dies. We know that. Oh, we profess they do and grieve at length because of it.

Yet they squirrel their way back . . . on their terms.

Ichabod elegiacally professed that Hannah—or Bernadette— gave birth to me in Portsmouth on the banks of the Ohio River, then drowned herself at its confluence with the Mississippi in Cairo's Little Egypt. Her white kerchief head covering lingering on the water's surface like a Christ lily.

I'm indebted to Ernest for framing her death in that manner. Suppose Billy Coombs had to wax eloquent? Except I've been given no choice as to when she appears before me, or in what guise. Same for Billy and Franz's German father: Onkel Jakob Bojangles.

The dead resurrect themselves within us.

* * *

Troubled that I was being ensnared into Ichabod's narrative, I left Berea for Portsmouth. He had begun to drop off library books to *"expand your intellectual horizons, Jeremiah."* Friends became less important as I sought escape in his favorite writers.

Kafka's narratives, then Sherwood Anderson's and Flannery O'Connor's. The first novel Ernest shared with me was Faulkner's *As I Lay Dying*.

I had begun living inside their minds instead of my own.

Billy Coombs didn't know what to make of it. Me holed up in the house reading. We were becoming even more estranged. Perhaps not to address the obvious, he spent more time with flour-white Magdalena.

The house I'd known since childhood was shared mostly by me and occasionally the ghosts of Eva, Chester, Hannah, and Onkel Jakob.

Mostly on Sunday, Ichabod—who, in truth, had become my best friend—would stop by to sit out on the porch and discuss what I was reading.

Remember how early on the neighbors said he was the "Son of Jesus"?

Well, I attribute my being rescued from the hegemony of religion and tribal prejudice to Ichabod Tyner, despite my not being totally convinced he wasn't my father.

PART TWO

"GOD DON'T EAT OKRA"

CHAPTER FIVE

Blacktown Portsmouth stood in stark contrast to my Berea neighborhood.

First off, the Roman Catholic church wasn't its epicenter. There were more houses of worship than corner stores: Big Bethel AME, Ebenezer, First African Baptist, Abyssinian Baptist, Bethel AME, First Missionary Baptist, Church of God in Christ, and the Mt. Olive Missionary.

On Lord's Day in Blacktown song and celebration erupted from its wood-framed worship houses. In contrast, neighbors headed down our street on Sunday to attend St. Andrews like they had no choice. Dire faces with offspring in tow unwitting to their being conditioned for a lifetime of penance. Parishioners successively kneeling and crossing themselves during Mass.

But there was no B-3 Hammond organ to spawn their gyrating. No chorus of *Amens* or *Hallelujahs* rising up to the echoless ceilings. No colossus rood of the Redeemer suspended in their modest bethels.

St. Andrews' priests didn't hoof it in their chasubles. Joy on this day there had been bartered for a Pope with carmine shoes, a fealty to piety and pomp, and a catechism inscribed by men.

In Blacktown Portsmouth I began to feel alive. Especially at Mt. Olive Missionary with my "cousins" whom heretofore I didn't even know existed. There the Hammond B-3 organ sung my soul . . . an experience I'd never encountered in all my eighteen years. It's the instrument that cousin Bennie played in the house where I stayed.

He'd first heard the B-3 at Mt. Olive. Imagine being inspired in church.

Growing up in Berea, I'd certainly been touched by the story of Jesus where I memorized the Beatitudes. *But contemplate memorizing the B-flat diminished chord on the Hamond B-3.* Accompanying a riotous "Steal Away Home," the sound transcended an orgasm. Why didn't it belong in church?

It's as if the father confessors at St. Andrews were teaching me and others the Stations of the Cross on how to die.

No Christly wonder why Billy Coombs chose to sleep in on Sundays.

* * *

The inclement night I arrived in Portsmouth, I knocked on the Sisters of Conscience convent door. A novice who greeted me evidenced no expression of surprise. She hung my wet coat in their mud room.

Soon sitting down to a cheese sandwich and glass of milk, Sister Alice began guessing my age then left to return with a black ledger. I watched her leaf through the pages until she rested her index finger on an inscription.

"Bernadette," she said.

At that very moment I was shaken by what must have been racing through my mother's mind when she was asked for her name at the convent's entry hall.

Would it be Hannah?

"Many of the offspring to the un-wed mothers we've ministered to over the years return like you, Jeremiah. Bernadette was without a home when she arrived and we provided her one. As we will with you."

That night I slept in a tiny attic that accommodated three spartan beds. The others were unoccupied except one.

He was half sitting up, eyeing me while resting on one arm.

"We get around, don't we, son?"

His handsaw hooked to the bed post.

"Your beloved grandmother asked me to look after you. It's the least I could do for her."

Onkel Jakob, dressed in a white cotton smock, climbed out of the covers and yanked the string connecting the single dormitory bulb. The moonlight piercing the one windowpane shaped in a triangle traced his tortured limp back to his bed.

* * *

One of several black nuns in the convent, Sister Alice had made it all possible. I had the good fortune to be assigned to Alsada's boarding house by her.

A century-old Victorian by the Baltimore & Ohio railroad tracks had an attic dormitory, too, but hers had twelve beds of different wood and brass vintages, each piled high with musty patchwork quilts of Joseph coat's pink, orange, red, yellow, copper, and purple.

Gibby and Onkel Jakob slept under the eaves in separate twins.

Myself, Esther, and Fern liked sleeping near the window so we could look out. Bennie was often absent: "I'm on the road a lot." Which I took to mean he slept in the skating rink where he played during the week . . . or more likely with one of the many young ladies who had become enamored by his Hammond B-3 alchemy.

The girl cousins and I were tempting adulthood. Having Jakob and Gibby situated in the room's darkest corner in a curious way became a soporific for our sleeping.

It was as if those two, softly chortling and palavering as they constantly did, kept our demons at bay. We found it comical how Onkel Jakob began to adapt Gibby's patois as his own. I can't recall a night when each of us, including her, didn't snicker as we watched

Jakob waddle out from under the covers to yank the string on the dormitory's single lightbulb.

It was the visualizing him waddle back to bed that delighted us most. For effect he'd oblige by rasping the dull teeth of his handsaw against his brass bed post, setting each of us on edge.

Over time I no longer anguished Messerschmitts whirling in my head. But an incident that occurred soon after I'd arrived at Alsada's, unsettled me even more.

* * *

DeForest Road was a medley of dissonance that July night.

White hoods had torched three creosote-impregnated crosses in a meadow across our road, and Aunt Alsada's devoted black friend and frequent boarder, Gibby, who lived by the railroad tracks, knelt paralyzed as her tar-paper shanty burned to the ground.

Long after dark, the attic floorboards creaked; Gibby was walking back and forth, quietly singing "Steal Away Home." From Bennie's new Hammond B-3 downstairs rose an electrifying "Night in Tunisia," and in their bedroom below us, Uncle Leonard—an African American—grunted bromides to Alsada's anguished sighs, while an engineer boarder on a layover from the Chesapeake & Ohio run tossed on the metal springs in his.

Then the Blue Zephyr to Cincinnati whined through the junction around midnight.

When Bennie began piping a mournful "Just A Closer Walk With Thee," I sensed the fiery crosses had unnerved him, too. Would the turnip hats return to torch the commodious Victorian in which we lay chasing sleep—while Gibby was stepping off to Galilee?

At cockcrow, we all gathered at the elephantine-legged kitchen table, watching Alsada attend sparking bacon and a heaping iron skillet of scrambled eggs on her kerosene stove. Gibby, who could've fit in an orange crate, sat at the table's head in Alsada's house dress, looking like she'd been draped in a courthouse flag. My adopted cousins, Fern and Esther, sat alongside. We bent over our plates, acting as if the woman had been residing in the Queen Anne boarding house with the family forever.

Until she began sobbing.

Alsada fingered her apron. "Weren't nothin' to do with you, Gibby. They weren't meanin' to get you."

The guest's ash-white braid swept pendulum-like over her chair's back.

"They be men, Gibby. You know about men? Emptier inside than a darning bole. Hollow like a drum. If you don't got no soul, you bellow. Howl to the moon like the dogs of hell they be. They weren't aimin' to get you . . . or me."

But Alsada was lying. What we witnessed the evening before had never befallen Portsmouth Junction.

"They *be* intendin' to get me, Miss Alsada. First the cross, dear Jesus, then my house."

Gibby stood and raised her arms to the ceiling like she was testifying.

"She lay outside last night," Alsada said, motioning to us sitting at the table.

"Yes, praise God, I did."

"Right under your window, Bennie."

"They ain't gittin' me there!" Gibby cried.

Bennie and I stared at his mother in disbelief. Directly under his bedroom window ran the open ditch alongside DeForest Road into which all the sewage waste of each residence discharged.

"It's where the poor soul hid." Alsada shook her head.

"They catch me anyplace else, hunt me down in my house, in the field, in the woods . . . but the white sheets don't dare lift me out of shit. Cause that be my grave . . . and praise Jesus I'm still here. Ain't that so, Miss Alsada?"

My aunt and her bereft neighbor exchanged a worried glance.

"Your mama bathed me. Your sweet mama who ain't brown or white, did so," Gibby said, pointing to Bennie.

That afternoon, he and I went to inspect Gibby's burned-out shanty. Its scant remains—an iron bed frame and springs scorched orange.

A pair of pearly string-laced heels she wore to church hung from a dogwood tree.

"It's those bastards' warning," Bennie spat.

"What'd she do?" I asked.

"Not be lard-white like me and Mama," he shrugged.

"Will those men come after your ma and Uncle Leonard?"

"They don't knock on your door and mercifully ask, you know."

"Would they torch our house?"

Bennie glumly nodded.

"Who are these men?"

"Come out of that tabernacle top the road," he said.

At the crest of DeForest Road where it joined the highway into Kentucky, stood a single-story, nondescript edifice with no windows and a double-door entrance painted jasmine.

The congregation's children all wore shiny red snare drums strapped bandolier-style to their chests, and women in white shirtwaist dresses hoisted rayon banners on flagstaffs. Except the opaline banners were blank. Soot-pocked men from the junction's roundhouse carried a motley array of band instruments, some silver and others brass, and blew an off-key "Old Rugged Cross."

They filed down the center of DeForest Road—not one member exchanged eye contact with the few of us lining the route—and at the tracks, marched back. The women, knees hoisting waist-high, stamped their heels explosively onto the hard pavement.

"What the hell was that all about?" Uncle Leonard asked Bennie and me from the deep shadows of the Victorian's porch.

Alsada, who was sitting embroidering on its oak swing, answered, "There's a storm a comin'. Dark one," she said, "brewin' over the meadow."

For days following the burning crosses and the torching of Gibby's abode, Bennie suffered the probable fate of his keyboard. At night when it was time to go to bed, he no longer slept upstairs.

"In the event," he explained.

"You gonna put the organ on your back and run up the road with it when the turnip hats arrive?" I scoffed.

"Don't know what I'll do. But in Christ's name, the bastards are gonna have to take us both . . . me and my B-3."

I envisioned vacuum tubes, pedals, levers, and ivory keys like Christmas ornaments decorating the maples out front of Aunt Alsada's house. The B-3's carcass gutted like Gibby's shack.

One full week after the Klan's mayhem—it was a Sunday afternoon—Bennie and I'd just returned from fishing at Mosquito Lake that lay a mile or so beyond the crossing. We'd brought home a raft of sunfish for frying up a lunch. Out back he chopped off the sunnies' heads on a millstone with a rusty hatchet.

It's when we heard the ragtag white band.

Gibby was sitting in my aunt's living room with the shades drawn, pretending she was reading the New Testament. But she knew its parables by heart. Uncle tinkered with their old Willys sedan in the garage.

Alsada looked up from her stove.

We all froze as the cacophonous "Onward Christian Soldiers" grew louder.

"They're comin' our way," she said dourly.

The *orkestra* halted directly in front of our house. Only the women with their staffs snapped to a surly command to face the Queen Anne. The gold-fringed banners were thrust out toward our porch as if words of dire warning were embossed on their fluttering raiment. The women sternly bore them in some ineluctable malediction while the snare drums beat a steady pulse.

Aunt Alsada watched from behind the front screen door. Inside the garaged Willys, Uncle Leonard spied through its rear-view mirror.

At the rear of the *orkestra*, and walking backward, an adipose male struck a bass drum mounted on a Radio Flyer wagon. A massive wine stain on the left-hand side of his face glowed each time the instrument's *boom* resonated through our rooms.

"It's the thundering over the meadow," Aunt Alsada said. She turned to Bennie. "Go tell Gibby to hide."

"Where?"

"The attic."

"*But my organ*!"

"I've got a plan," she said. "Wait till dark."

At my aunt's bidding, Bennie and I cloaked Gibby in Uncle Leonard's raven overcoat and fedora, ushered her up the wide stairway to the second landing, then onto the very narrow ladder to the unfinished attic.

Gibby sat on its iron bed that was piled high with musty quilts and began rocking back and forth, chanting to herself.

She's going to walk to Galilee for certain this night, I thought.

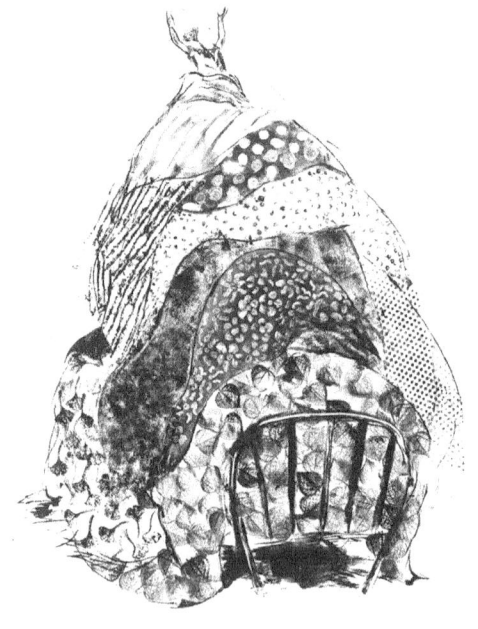

None of us ate the chopped-head sunnies that afternoon, but sat in the dusky living room quietly vigilant. Bennie pulled the plug on his B-3 and shrouded it with a blanket. In the gloom it looked as if we were attending a wake. The covered bier sat in the corner under a picture of the *Gainsborough Boy*. Periodically our guest's haunted droning pierced the boarding house's sepulchre air.

Once night began to engulf the room, and we could no longer make out each other's faces, Alsada spoke. "The fish bellies are assembling behind the copse of birch trees in the meadow. Now listen to me closely."

Within minutes Bennie and I were shouldering, with Uncle Leonard's assist, the Hammond B-3 onto the front porch, attaching it with a chain of extension cords to the living room's sole electric outlet.

"Now go up and fetch Gibby."

Alsada had Gibby sit between Uncle Leonard and me on the umber sofa while she accompanied Bennie upstairs.

When they reappeared, each was dressed in Sabbath whites. Aunt had fashioned a paperboard crown on her head flecked with silver that sparkled in the amber glow from a hurricane lantern.

She handed Bennie a sheet of music and directed him to "Play as if yours and Gibby's life depended upon it. Like you are in church," she said. "Except you've never been. But you got a fertile imagination, boy."

First Bennie made his mummer's entrance onto the porch and took a seat at the B-3.

Within moments, it was as if a cathedral Wurlitzer were pealing mellifluous strains of "Nearer My God To Thee" over the entire Ohio valley. My cousin keyed and pedaled the hymn with God-fearing fervor.

Then out strode Aunt Alsada, an imposing materfamilias costumed in liquidly white rayon, including white hose and string shoes with her mystical cardboard crown glittering silver in the nickel-plated skylight.

Down the front steps she tramped, halting at the odious ditch where she snapped about-face and gestured solemnly toward our house. The screen door creaked open. Draped in Uncle's mourning weeds and brandishing, scepter-like, a knurled cane, Gibby rambled barefoot to the lugubrious dirge with second-line pluck while trailing my buxom aunt onto the center of the road.

At the hymn's chorus, Uncle Leonard funereally backed the Willys out of the gravel driveway. Black crepe paper lined all its windows except the windshield. He turned as if heading to the highway, but braked at the scorched meadow.

Aunt Alsada pivoted once again. She briskly saluted our crossing's Grand Panjandrum, then drew the melancholy friend tightly to her bosom, lingering there, before opening the shrouded sedan's rear door. Gibby, whose pearly heels lay on its floorboard, bowed, discreetly returned the Dobbs, and climbed into the backseat with my aunt slipping in beside her.

Uncle Leonard laid on his horn, shoved the Willys into gear, and crept up DeForest Road.

Cousin Bennie segued into a smoking "Steal Away Home."

CHAPTER SIX

After the Tabernacle *Orkestra* incident, the dark-skinned twins began referring to Onkel Jakob and me as their "Honky Berea" blood relatives.

Once the dormitory light was extinguished, it was irreverent Fern who'd request one of us put on a Klan show. "Scare the bejesus out of me, please!" In return, she'd promise she and her sister would perform an African dance. Which I had reason to believe—having now bunked alongside the girls for a couple weeks—they'd cavort nude in the Gibbous moon illuminating our triangle window.

It wasn't the first time I had been sexually aroused by them.

A week after my having been put up in Aunt Alsada's dormitory, one of them slid alongside me in bed—then I was unable to tell which—whispering I'd have to undergo an "inspection" if I wanted to stay. She pulled me out of bed to stand between her and her twin who was stationed in the darkest corner of the attic shining a pen flashlight into my eyes.

I know it now was Fern who spoke. "Repeat after me: *Credo quia absurdum est.*"[14]

"*Credo quia absurdum est.*"

Fern summarily yanked my pajama bottoms to the plank floor. They both stared as Esther shined the flashlight onto my genitals. On cue they burst out in laughter.

_____

14 *"I Believe Because It Is Absurd"*

Humiliated, I angrily chastised them for awaking Onkel Jakob.

Fern asked if I wanted to join their *African Order of Tertullian*?

"If you turn out the flashlight . . . yes."

She pulled up my bottoms and kissed me sweetly on the cheek. "We laughed, Jeremiah, not at what we saw . . . but because of what a Honky cousin expected we black-ass twins might do. No offense."

I had come to love these cheeky young women.

Perceiving that there was much I didn't know or understand, the twins took it upon themselves to enlighten me as Ichabod had endeavored to do. What I admired so about the pair is that they indulged my conviction that Onkel Jakob had shadowed me to Portsmouth. That, indeed, he was as "in the flesh real" as was I and each of them along with aged Gibby.

In truth, the dormitory in Aunt Alsada's century-old Victorian had metamorphosed into our academy.

"I Believe Because It Is Absurd" the twins needle-worked into each of our pillow cases.

There wasn't any subject we didn't take seriously.

Especially our white-hooded neighbors who resided on Blacktown's edge.

* * *

Soon after I arrived at Alsada's, one night when we all gathered around her commodious lion paw's oak table for supper, I watched her nudge Uncle Leonard when we were all seated.

"Jeremiah," he smiled. "Do you know whose seat you have taken?"

Fern and Esther acted as if they weren't listening.

I jumped up. "Oh, I'm very sorry," and looked around to see who was waiting to sit down.

Alsada laughed. "It's only because we recall your mother sitting in that very same spot the months she spent living with us prior to your birth. It struck your uncle and me as if you somehow knew."

The thoughts in my head began colliding.

"Hannah?"

"We took to her immediately. Didn't we, Leonard?"

Fern chimed in, laughing. "Mama is white folks just like you, Jeremiah."

Leonard suppressed a grin. "It's only because they have grown to like you, son. Some of our guests haven't been so honored."

"And my mother?"

"We didn't want her to leave," Alsada replied.

The exchange between us at the table ceased as if a timer had rung.

Gibby, who generally kept to herself, vacated the table and headed back upstairs. Her food had barely been touched.

"Perhaps one day Gibby will open up to you," Alsada explained. "There's a reason you are occupying Sister Hannah's chair."

The twins and Uncle Leonard nodded in agreement.

I was no longer hungry either.

She was sitting on her dormitory bed, an open Bible on her lap. The twins remained downstairs.

"Gibby, please tell me about her."

Like I wasn't there. I could have been Onkel Jakob.

"Look," I said, "I've never seen or spoken to her. We all have mamas, Gibby. I want to know why."

She reflexively leafed through the worn *Holy Writ's* pages.

"Why all of a sudden did you up from the dinner table and leave?"

Gibby wore the same pained expression that morning when she spoke of her escape from the Klan in the DeForest Road open sewer. Eyeing me like she was trying to read my heart, she muttered: "Your mama wanted to go home, Jeremiah."

I wasn't understanding.

"It's why she trekked all the way here, seeking where she lived."

Gibby rose from her bed and shuffled to the dormitory window, before turning. "We thought she'd found it here. Until the night we were told they'd discovered her body on the banks of the Mississippi near Little Egypt.

"She had written a note to me at this address: '*Until we meet again at the river. Hannah.*'"

I lay down on my bed.

Momentarily I heard Gibby prating from the dark under the eaves. It sounded as if she were giving Onkel Jakob directions to Mount Olive on Elm Street.

* * *

In the days following, I was able to gather some additional information about the two women. But mostly it was anodyne. Seems Alsada and the rest, especially the twins, suspected some dark secret had passed between Hannah and her Black friend as their beds stood an arm's length apart in the dormitory.

Yet, nothing. Even when I prodded Fern or Esther to guess.

Until one early morning I awoke, startled to see Gibby standing at the foot of my bed. She handed me an envelope, the greeting card kind, with its address scratched out. It felt as if it contained a piece of cloth instead of paper.

Gibby shook her head like I wasn't to open it in her presence.

"It's a piece of your mother. I give it to you in her name."

I listened to Gibby pad down the stairs with no shoes. She would collect them at the front door on her way out to prayer service.

The envelope lay unopened until later that day when the dormitory was vacant. Inside was a cotton facsimile of the yellow Star of David badge inscribed with "*Juif.*" On its reverse, "*Hannah*" sewn with white thread. Distraught, I clutched it in the palm of my hand that burned like it had been branded.

For no earthly reason, I envisioned Ichabod standing by the triangle window glass, watching me. "What do you want me to say?" I cried, and slid the yellow badge back into Gibby's envelope.

But then saw it shining on the left side of Ichabod's breast.

* * *

That night and for several consecutive ones, my Berea benefactor made an appearance in my dreams. Always mute but staring at me intently.

Most troubling was Gibby's distancing from me. In the dormitory she would go out of her way so as to avoid our meeting. As if to her I was now simply another guest of Aunt Alsada's who was passing through.

Yet Onkel Jakob and she were still close.

If anything, their nocturnal exchanges in the ink-black dormitory became more animated. She spoke in tongues as far as I could determine. He, on the other hand, in fractured English.

The humor had worn off for the twins.

Once after midnight, Fern came to my bed and queried, "Why, in jesusname, did you bring him along, Jeremiah?" Except she was smart enough not to await for an answer. Each of us had an *other* who shared our bed. I empathized with her frustration, because Onkel Jakob never slept. And Gibby was the only soul in Aunt Alsada's house who listened to him.

There was the incident when just before the dormitory light was to be extinguished, she gathered before our beds and announced that Onkel Jakob and she would entertain us with a little vignette.

"He will narrate while I act out what he says."

Gibby disappeared into the dormitory's shadows of which there were a multitude.

Within moments we watched her carry a dusty old valise back and forth in front of the room's only window. She appeared shaken, frightened actually, and kept looking behind her as if she were being followed.

Once again she disappeared to return with yet another worn valise, and repeated the same motions as earlier. Only her anxiety had ratcheted up, *unnerved by heeltaps striking the cobblestones, erupting like paper caps, approaching from behind . . . inclined neither to look up nor over her shoulder.*

Again and again this scene kept repeating itself in a speeded up fashion. The battered abandoned valises accumulated before the triangle glass pane, each in my mind at least, suggesting the missing owner who had failed to escape.

Where Gibby had found these props I could only venture to

guess that she had collected them from the Sisters of Conscience convent, having been abandoned by their owners.

Finally we heard Onkel Jakob's voice emanate from some dark niche in the dormitory.

"It's the night of broken glass," he intoned.

Gibby reappeared garbed in white, carrying her own satchel.

She walked to the single overhead light in the dormitory and pulled its string.

Then in total darkness we heard glass breaking, shards tinkling on the bare wooden floor, accompanied by Onkel Jakob crying: "All aboard!"

Gibby begins caroling:

> I am traveling on the hallelujah line,
> On the good old Gospel train,
> I am on the right track and never will go back
> To the station of sin again.
> I need no fare, I'm riding on a pass,
> 'Tis the blood for sinners slain,
> I am traveling on the hallelujah line,
> On the good old Gospel train.

In her addled brain, Hannah's confidant was hell-bent on redeeming Onkel Jakob from perdition.

* * *

Several days later in the middle of the night one of the twins cried out:

"God don't eat Okra!"

Gibby shot upright in her bed. "Quiet!" she bellowed in Onkel Jakob's voice.

The three of us were now rolling over with delight.

Thus commenced a protracted period where none of us wanted to miss what would randomly transpire each night in the dormitory.

From the outset of my stay at Alsada's, it was apparent that she, Gibby, was succumbing to mental instability. Her narratives were increasingly fractured. And, not the least of it, was her weaving Onkel Jakob into her storyline. Like he had become her long-lost paramour despite the constant grievance he caused her.

Except it was *I* who had introduced him to her and the twins.

Overtime it became clear to me that Gibby's sibling-like relationship with Hannah *was* the basis for her adopting Onkel.

The second dusk of our dormitory revelry, Fern asked Gibby where she first learned that God didn't like Okra.

"Sister Hannah," she replied.

"Where do you think she first learned it?" Esther chimed in.

With the half-light still illuminating our beds, Gibby reached under her pillow and held up two books, each with a plethora of dog-eared pages. I climbed out of bed and asked if I could look at them.

"Read 'em," she replied. "Will do you good." Then pointed to the twins. "You, too. Time you learned some truth!"

It provoked our chortling once again.

Turns out we began absorbing many of the underlined passages from *Jonah's Gourd Vine* and *Their Eyes Were Watching God,* written in the late 1930s by Zora Neale Hurston and narrated in Black vernacular.

When the twins shared the hardbacks, Gibby handed me another: *Cane,* a novel published in 1923 by African American poet and novelist Jean Toomer. "Here, Jeremiah, given your fancy for jazz."

We already had been reading each night prior to turning in for a couple of weeks. Fern had insisted. But the books she'd brought back from the library were all nonfiction texts principally centered around their African ancestry.

But after several hours of reading on successive evenings in the dormitory now, something had changed. Ironically Gibby, through these two Black writers, had become our instructor.

It was as if the young women were discovering their real selves in the lyricism of Black speech.

And in doing so, Gibby was being resurrected.

Each sundown in our dormitory sessions, she played a larger role as nighttime stealthily entered. We were slowly relinquishing our reasoning to a darker more poetic mystery. As if personalities, the likes of which we hadn't heretofore encountered, were emerging out of these texts that Hannah had gifted Gibby.

Indeed, it felt as if the characters in these novels had moved into the dormitory alongside us to occupy the eight beds left vacant.

This was especially true for Fern and Esther. The novels were functioning as a polishing stone, mitigating the more abrasive aspects of the twins' personalities. Each had become less sure of herself, evidencing a palpable sorrow that I hadn't seen earlier.

They had come in contact with a mother and aunts they had never known.

Gibby was too far removed from reality now for her to serve as the medium to what had been lost of their identity.

Yet each twin now held her in abeyance. They swallowed their laughter when her words provoked it.

I followed their lead . . . or endeavored to.

It seemed the greater appreciation the three of us bestowed upon these works as our treasured ones, the more Gibby emerged as our dormitory seer, often opening our evening assemblage with an African American proverb or snippets of what she recalled from Hurston and Toomer.

Like the half-light she ran between the twins' beds, caroling:

"Wisht Ah had uh needle Fine ez Ah could sew Ah'd sew mah baby to my side And down de road Ah'd go . . . Down de road baby Down de road baby It's killing mama Oh, it's killing mama. Too hot for words."[i]

Then halting at mine: *"Ain't no use askin' the cow to pour you a glass of milk."[ii]*

But it was Gibby's longing that wove through her performances those evenings. It spoke of a melody that she could no longer remember. *"What's beauty anyway but ugliness if it hurts you,[iii]* Onkel

Jakob?" Her mournful bitterness reverberated off the dormitory walls, causing the three of us to shudder in our beds.

It often felt as if Gibby had pulled out from under her bed a valise of time from which her memories had fled, leaving but a moth's dust she could draw from.

What she always remembered, however, was "Long John," the spiritual she celebrated in the church aisles as a young woman. The three of us would leap out of our beds and clap in time to her singing at the top of her lungs while parading about the dormitory.

It's a long John, He's a long gone, Like a turkey through the corn, Through the long corn.

Well, my John said, In the ten chap ten, "If a man die, He will live again."
Well, they crucified Jesus And they nailed him to the cross; Sister Mary cried, "My child is lost!"
    Well, long John, He's long gone, He's long gone. Mister John, John, Old Big-eye John, Oh, John, John, It's a long John.
Says-uh: "Come on, gal, And-uh shut that do'," Says, "The dogs is comin' And I've got to go."
    It's a long John, He's long gone, It's a long John, He's a long gone.
"Well-a two, three minutes, Let me catch my win'; In-a two, three minutes, I'm gone again."
    He's long John, He's long gone, He's long gone, He's long gone.
Well, my John said Just before he did, "Well, I'm goin' home, See Mary Lid."
    He's John, John, Old John, John, With his long clothes on, Just a-skippin' through the corn.
Well, my John said On the fourth day, Well, to "tell my rider That I'm on my way."
    He's long gone, He's long gone, He's long gone, It's a long John.
"Gonna call this summer, Ain't gon' call no mo', If I call next summer, Be in Baltimore." He's long gone. [iv]

The twins and I committed the spiritual to memory, and even

when Gibby was too exhausted to join in, we ended each of our dormitory sessions singing and dancing prior to pulling the bulb's string off for the night.

At dinner late one afternoon, all of us around the table, Aunt Alsada asked, "Sounds like you are having too much fun up there dusk time and later. What are you all up to?"

Gibby didn't even lift an eyebrow.

"Oh, nothing." Fern and Esther responded simultaneously.

Uncle Leonard spoke up. "I'm hearing a jubilation parade about your beds. You two the chorus. Miss Gibby leading you on."

Esther asked her mother to pass the sweet potatoes. The conversation was dropped.

But my hosts had to notice the change in their longest boarder. Earlier her rapid mental decline triggered shared looks of concern about the table. What piqued their attention now was the attire she wore for dinner.

A faded wedding dress . . .

None of us said a word.

Until the evening Aunt Alsada took it upon herself to inquire. "Gibby, when will you invite the gentleman to dinner so we can meet him?" Seemed like minutes passed before she raised her head:

"The rainbow might be better lookin' if 'twasn't such a cheap show."

Fern, giggling and coughing, spit a mouthful of milk down her shirtwaist.

"What's his name?" Esther teased.

"Jakob," Gibby replied nonplussed. "Most of the time he's after whut he kin git, then he's gone like a turkey through the corn."ᵛ

There wasn't a dry eye at the table that night. Gibby was born anew on the hastening eve of her death. The three of us especially knew *he* resided under the eaves in the dormitory waiting her out.

Her real paramour.

Onkel Jakob couldn't compete.

CHAPTER SEVEN

"Love makes your soul crawl out from its hiding place." vi

Unexpectedly, Fern and I grew closer during this period we recognized as Gibby's final days.

The onset of death's appearance caused us to step livelier. Levitated by "Long John," Gibby and her shadow patterned the dormitory's plank floors and walls.

There were moments I wondered if I was even alive.

But it was Fern's initial dismissal of me that provoked my interest in her.

Unlike her sister, she wore her feelings like beetles pinned to her blouse and delighted in teasing they be provoked. At which point she'd prick you with more.

Then laugh, of course, to erase any intended offense.

But what was it about Jeremiah from Berea that set her off?

Perhaps her whispering "Polly wants a cracker" when she passed my bed at night. Only Esther would giggle. It took me a couple dark hours to catch on. That's when I grabbed her sleeping gown when she swooped by.

"You don't like crackers?" I asked.

"If he peddlin' watermelon sugar, I jes might," she japed, yanking out of my grip.

I'd no idea what she meant.

"But words is like the spots on dice: no matter how y fumbles em, there's times when they jes wont come."vii Fern outwitted me too often.

All the while as Gibby had begun to unveil her soul.

It all commenced the eve I asked her about her children . . . not knowing if she had any.

"A son."

"What's his name?"

"He ain't no more."

Fern shot me a glance, cautioning me to stop.

"Tobias. Named after his daddy. Figured if one left, there 'id still be another hangin' round. 'Cept they both gone."

A pall crept over the dormitory. Nightfall was coming on too soon it seemed. The twins picked up their books to resume reading. But Gibby had begun the story telling. "You want to know how my boy Tobias died?" I lingered at the foot of her bed.

"Ask Onkel Jakob," she said, gesturing to under the eaves. "He knows damn well how my boy died. Don't ya!" She'd stood up shaking her fist. "Tell 'em Onkel what you did. Go on!"

The twins became unnerved by Gibby's vehemence.

"He don't want to speak it, do he? Can't, becauses it catches in his throat. He want to choke to death. Ain't it the truth? Then maybe I tell 'em what you did.

"Tobias was standin' at our window one evening waiting for his father to come home from work. Just like he did every night. And this evenin' my young'un was dressed up in a uniform. Army corporal he called himself. Had carved a rifle out of an old hickory tree limb.

"Wanted his daddy to see how he'd grown. Practicin' salutes in the big old flaking silver mirror in our bedroom.

"And this particular evenin' his daddy came home, took Tobias up the stairs. Says he wanted to stand alongside him in the big old mirror.

"I asked why.

"To see what's missing," he said.

"Then I heard him ask my boy to remove his uniform. Lay his

rifle on the bed. Then silence. That's when an angry old wind began howlin' outside the house.

"A loud crash of glass bursting. Like the mirror had been tossed down the stairs. Our bedroom window had been attacked by that large black crow in the hikry tree.

"Then I seen Tobias's boy uniform climb down the steps without him.

"And walkin' out the frond door . . .

"He's long gone, He's long gone, He's long gone.
"With his long clothes on, Just a-skippin' through the corn."

Gibby lay back down, drawing the quilt up to her neck as pitch black bathed our beds.

* * *

So, for several intense story-book weeks in the dormitory, we were family with deranged Gibby becoming our mother and by default Onkel Jakob, her eidolon philanderer husband, our father. Fortuitously, he was mostly out for the evening . . . except when he wasn't.

Those were the terrifying nights the twins and I shared one bed.

He'd mark the late hour with his tap cleats as he struggled up the dormitory steps. Gibby, ashier than the ghost of Lazarus, speaking in tongues Christ couldn't even decipher.

Now, women forget all those things they don't want to remember, and remember everything they don't want to forget . . . Then they act and do things accordingly."viii

The twins and I could only imagine what brought on Gibby's spells. Whether Tobias Sr. owned tapping shoes or not, she clearly fetched that Onkel Jakob had, plus that he fired up lust in her inner organs like old Tobias never could. With me lying skin-close between each of the girls, we witnessed Gibby dressed in a man's coal-black suit and tap shoes, clinging like a forsaken lover to her wedding gown stuffed with crow's feathers to commence the *Danse Macabre*.

We only saw her enact it twice.

It was this time—the second—that chilled each of our souls to their earthern core.

Gibby in preparation for the cleat tapping in Alsada's upper room, had lit incense that wafted a fresh loam bouquet. She outlined a circle of votive candles about her betrothal bed. Once the tapping on the steps commenced, out of the darkness appears the "couple" . . . high stepping to a festive second-line rendition of "Just A Closer Walk With Thee." Onkel plucks a black rose out of his suit coat lapel and pins it on the breast of the wedding dress. He dances it to the illuminated bed, chorusing:

Just a closer walk with Thee,
Grant it, Jesus, is my plea,

Daily walking close to Thee
Let it be, dear Lord, Let it be.

Then thrusts the bridal gown onto the bed and crawls on top. The music stops.

Gibby removes her suit coat and trousers, and lies alongside her gown adorned by the black rose.

Onkel Jakob, did you love her like you do me?
Did you walk her along the River Jordan like you once did me?
Did you sing her alive under her bridal lace like you once did me?
Oh, dear Lord, Dear Lord, Let it be. Let it be.
Where does the Corpse Road lead, Mr. Tapman?
Where does the Corpse Road lead?

In her nightgown, Gibby cradles the stuffed bridal gown in her arms and hangs it above the dormitory stairway. *"Keep an eye out for him,"* she calls out from her bed. The candles have now died.

He'll be wearing a black rose in his lapel. They grow alongside River Jordon on the Corpse Road.
He always comes callin' after dark.

Fern, Esther, and I in one bed eventually fell asleep until dawn.

* * *

"I come back to tell you, brother, that white faces are petals of roses. That dark faces are petals of dusk."[ix]

Fern, quoting from *Cane* one evening, was my first indication that she had begun to unveil her fancy for me. Despite our growing friendship, at bottom I believed she viewed me a Berea cracker deficient in the brainpower she and her twin displayed.

Maybe her lamp was lit when the three of us lay alongside each other.

Mine, of course, burned votive-orange soon after we met.

Perhaps something else was going on: one day I would depart Alsada's boardinghouse. And early on I witnessed Fern gingerly setting herself apart from the family. Despite her and Esther exiting Alsada's womb entwined, she was planting seeds of departure, cloaking the activity by her playful outspokenness and acerbic wit.

So, from the first night I slept in one of the twelve dormitory beds, it was hers that illuminated a pathway to mine. I just had to wait for the petal of dusk to unfold.

On a premonition, and long after we all turned in, one night I lay alongside her.

It was as if she had been lying awake anticipating my visit.

The dormitory was stygian black.

"How did you find me?" She grinned. "You bein' the only one of us three who can't hide in the dark."

"The persimmon tree's scent," I said. "Don't need no light to find you. Words neither."

"Pungent and composite, the smell of farmyards is the fragrance of the woman. She does not sing; her body is a song. She is in the forest, dancing."[x] Maybe you be forgettin' Jean Toomer, Jeremiah."

Fern sat straight up in bed, holding back from laughing in my face.

"You get that, white boy? *The smell of farmyards be the fragrance of the woman.* Persimmon blossoms grow on the tongues of Berea poets, do they?"

I shoved her back down on the bed as she pulled me along with her, whispering: "Work on it, kid. Maybe one day I'll lay a white rose on my black breast to surprise you." She cast a glance at Esther's bed, concerned that she may have awakened, then eyed me with reproach.

"Or perhaps you one of those *'who wishes to ripen a growing thing too soon'?*"

Those very words also left their mark on me when I read *Cane*.

As did Toomer's admonitory *"Wishes only make you restless."* I mutely bid Fern "Goodnight" and slipped back into my own bed.

But the next morning I overhead the twins arguing. Esther obviously hadn't been asleep.

"Fern, you make like you're turnin' 'gainst me," she cried.

One of the few times I hadn't experienced a Fern riposte.

"What you believe you saw, sister, didn't come from me or him. Suppose he had climbed alongside *you* last night."

"No crackers in my bed!" Esther sneered, to Fern's amusement, while sweeping her hand over her quilt.

Except we were no longer brother and sisters. Nor for the duration of our time together in Alasada's boarding house did the three of us share a bed again.

Esther had caught wind of our transgression.

It could all be traced back to Hannah. And Billy Coombs.

Chastened by Esther's rebuke, Fern willfully kept our distance in the dormitory. One day I shadowed her to a convenience store, hoping to engage.

Spotting me, she reacted with such fury I concluded it was time to leave Portsmouth, and returned to Alsada's to pack my belongings. In riled haste I was unaware of Fern standing alongside her bed watching me. Esther and Gibby were not present.

"Where do you think you're going, Whitebread?"

Still smoldering, I merely shrugged.

"Someplace sunnier than Blacktown?"

I wasn't about to engage in her ridicule.

Fern approached and sat down on my bed.

"You have never lived with anybody you loved, have you? Just those that have taken refuge in your head. Like your mother, Hannah, correct? She was never real was she? Except how you imagined her touching you as a child. It's why you followed her here, isn't it? To see if you could caress her back to life even if it was just some old memory she'd left behind for you to cherish the rest of your white rose days.

"What don't you understand about *dusk and hurt*, boy?

"You think I want to cause my sister's heart to bleed because of you? That wound 'id last a lifetime. Hurts in one's head . . . Jesus answers those.

"You followin' me to the store . . . what did you want me to say? 'Oh, Christ yes, let's run off and undress'? Is that what you're after? Well, let's get over that right now."

Fern stood and stripped down to her white cotton panties. Then even slipped out of those.

Like an ebony statue she stood erect before me.

Her eyes on fire.

"Do you want to touch any part of it, boy?"

"You come all the way down from Berea to see it, whiff it, right?

"Sure as hell ain't no possum apple, 'ya think?"

I picked up her clothes from the floor and handed them to her.

"Didn't mean no harm to you, Fern. You just happened to touch me new. That's all."

As she began dressing, I turned my head and returned packing.

But dazzling in my mind was her standing alongside me nude. The persimmons' creamy-white bell-shaped flower with four re-curved petals gliding down to her narrow feet. *That's what you will carry with you*, I thought.

Wishes only make you restless.

Fern softened. "I've a question, Jeremiah."

I stopped folding my clothes.

"What were you planning to do about Onkel Jakob?"

She watched me struggle to respond.

"Were you thinking you'd leave him here for Gibby? Except we both know where she's headed. *Don't we?*"

"Maybe he belongs to her now, Fern."

"Except dead folk depart empty. No place here in the dormitory for Onkel Jakob to be sleepin' 'n roamin' around once she dead . . . with you gone. Can you imagine *him* showin' up at Alsada's groanin' board?"

She burst out laughing.

"You best be packin' more than your clothes, Whitebread."

Fern walked to the stairway door, where the memory of Gibby's pellucid wedding dress hung listless, and turned facing me.

"Or waiting a bit longer until I be able to help."

Her voice . . . not mine to which I'd become so enamored.

She gave me no choice.

CHAPTER EIGHT

One week later, the twins and I were abruptly awakened in the middle of the night by an apparition floating inside the dormitory alongside our beds.

Gibby, in her wedding gown, was drumming on her Sunday-go-to-meetin' hatbox—attached to her chest by a rope cincture—declaiming *Jonah's Gourd Vine* dirge:

> *On the pale white horse of Death. On the cold icy hands of Death. On the golden streets of glory. Of Amen Avenue. Of Halleluyah Street . . . They beat upon the O-go-doe, the ancient drum. O-go-doe, O-go-doe, O-go-doe! . . . Not the little drum of kid-skin, for that is to dance with joy and to call to mind birth and creation, but O-go-doe, the voice of Death— that promises nothing, that speaks with tears only, and of the past.*[xi]

A dearth of recognition as she waved her arms over each of the twins. Until she paused alongside me. The drumming ceased.

"I'm leaving to meet Hannah." Gibby spoke as if I were a child.

"Wouldn't you like to come?" I had to lower my eyes as the madness in hers unnerved me.

"*O-go-doe, O-go-doe*" she sang like a nursery rhyme.

Then placed the hat box upon my bed, gesturing that I open it. Fern nodded that I must oblige. Folded inside lay a brown habit and a black veil alongside a distressed leather Sisters of Conscience breviary.

"*O-go-doe*, Child, Mama's callin' you. Come along with me and Onkel Jakob. We're meetin' Hannah in Little Egypt where the mighty Ohio weds the Mississippi. *O-go-doe*, you can ride on the pale white Horse of Death on Halleluyah Street. You mustn't tarry now.

"Minutes are a wastin'. Horse of Death is restless."

Gibby cautiously replaced the lid over my mother's habit and daily prayers, and resumed drumming. She stopped just outside the dormitory entryway.

"Onkel Jakob!" she cried. "*O-go-doe*, we must awaken all below."

I could swear I heard his tap shoes marking time down the steps. We listened to her knocking on Alsada's bedroom door. It was several moments before Esther spoke up.

"It's begun," she solemnly pronounced.

"Gibby's goin' home."

Yet the following evening at the dinner table, it appeared that nothing had changed. Gibby was reticent as common but finishing everything on her plate. The twins and I kept up a light conversation mostly to masque the obvious.

But there was melancholy in the air. An ending of sorts. Or perhaps a painful recognition that shortly one of the table chairs would be vacant.

A lifetime of memories evanesced.

Gibby's body no longer lying in the sewer ditch, but now within days graced in her wedding gown blanketed by loam. And Onkel Jakob following me home.

O-go-doe, Christ Jesus. O-go-doe.

* * *

The next morning after the twins departed the dormitory, I approached Gibby's bed. All her belongings were packed in paper grocery sacks on her made bed. She sat staring off in space.

"Dear Gibby, is there anything more to tell me about Hannah?" She mechanically gestured that the hatbox belonged to me. "I'm grateful," I said.

"He profaned what's inside."

"Who?"

"Onkel Jakob."

I heard a wooden cleat tap the floor alongside my bed. It was Onkel sitting in a straight-back chair with his hat on and a satchel on his lap, waiting. He was adamantly shaking his head.

"Who else, Gibby?"

"Billy Coombs."

"What did Mother confide in you?"

Like the words had desecrated themselves. "It was after dark. Two men were outside the parish house drinking. Bernadette entered St. Andrews to recite her evening prayers. Billy attacked her in the nave. Onkel Jakob looked on."

It was at that very moment when I personally drew a darker inference to what Gibby had gifted me:

The facsimile of the yellow Star of David badge with "Juif" inscribed inside. On its reverse, "Hannah" sewn with white thread in her hand.

A Jewess in Christ's house got what she deserved.

* * *

For several days after, Gibby and I were sharing the same cell, staring out at a fog-laden meadow empty of any signs of life.

Waiting.

Onkel Jakob had not stirred from his chair. The packed valise sitting urn-like on his legs. Even his wooden taps had ceased marking time.

Periodically a faint apparition of Billy Coombs crossed my vision. His face marked by red splotches of remorse. The shade of the imaginary scapular I'd placed over Hannah's torso.

Then he would disappear as rapidly, contrition for what he had done.

All our Berea's neighbors knew about it. How could they not have?

Why didn't I?

Was she ushered into either Padre Tom or Jerry's limousine that very night and driven to Portsmouth? Or maybe to Youngstown and dropped off at the Greyhound bus station?

I was not even privy to the unseemly rumors as to why Sister Bernadette, a.k.a. Hannah, had chosen to pay visit to her old neighborhood. To purge the sullied granite sanctuary steps by a rigorous scrubbing with soap and water, the parishioners banded together prior to Sunday Mass.

Before dawn the next morning, a sudden rainstorm alarmed each of us awake. It was the first time in the dormitory that I'd experienced wind penetrating the enclosure. Our shoes began to skate over the floor. The wooden chair in which Onkel had sat the previous night had blown over on its side. Gibby's hatbox lay open with Hannah's convent belongings scattered across the room.

I jumped out of bed to determine the storm's breach.

But immediately saw that one of the panes in the dormitory's window was missing. Rivulets of rainwater coursed under our beds toward Gibby's. Within moments I stood helpless witnessing the remaining glass being ominously drummed on by what sounded like hail before crashing at my feet.

"Oh-go-doe, Lord!" Gibby cried out.

Naked and with her arms outstretched, she raced into the rainstorm's onslaught. Countless spears of glass scatted across our room. The downpour washing over her feet began to turn crimson. Now the twins and I warily treaded across the floor to restrain the woman. Except, the thunderclaps and shattering glass had cloaked her in a rapturous embrace. Oblivious to our presence, at the dormitory's breached opening, she continued to wail,

"Oh-go-doe, Lord. Oh-go-doe. I'm returnin' home."

Esther yelled "No!"

Bolts of lightening illuminated her wizened brown body in a series of images flashed upon our walls moments before the arms dropped to its sides as she collapsed.

The twins knelt alongside.

Both girls—no, they were women now—removed their pajama tops and wrapped Gibby's feet, prior to carrying her back to her bed where they swaddled her in a white sheet. As if it had all been rehearsed, ritual like, in their heads. Neither cried.

Fern asked me to alert Aunt Alsada.

"Once I pick up my mother's belongings off the floor," I replied.

Gibby's wedding gown was part of the detritus, including the soaking wet habit and black veil splintered with glass. The dormitory room sanctuary-still as if the Horse of Death had poked its head in the shattered window.

Dawn light rose across Gibby's bier.

* * *

At dinner that evening an empty place setting marked Gibby's absence. Not a single word was exchanged. At its close, Alsada stood and asked when I planned to leave.

Neither twin raised her head.

"We've all enjoyed your presence here, Jeremiah. Please let us hear from you."

I nodded that I would.

Then as if to assuage my feelings of being asked to go, Alsada eyed Fern. They had obviously conferred earlier.

"I'm closing the boardinghouse, Jeremiah. *For now anyway.* Our table is too small to accommodate the memories of those who once sat here. Some never leave . . . like your mother and Gibby. It's time we let them go." She and Leonard left the room.

As Esther began to clear the table, Fern gestured that I follow her outside. We sat on the porch railing. "Where are you headed?" she asked.

"Don't know."

"Back to Berea?"

"Already left there."

Fern smiled like it was what she wanted to hear.

"Do you have money?"

"Enough to get me about as far as Hannah did." I laughed.

She looked about to see if no one was in earshot. "Esther agreed to attend a church gathering tonight in honor of Gibby. I'll meet you after dark in the dormitory. We'll plan on leavin' together before daybreak."

"Where are we going?"

"Ain't it enough we are?"

* * *

Mostly elderly women coifed in their Sunday best occupied the pews. I sat in the very last one and spotted Esther several rows ahead of me.

The choir, with Hammond organ accompaniment, began the service with "Closer My God To Thee." At the hymn's close, random members of the congregation remained standing and spoke poignantly in the decedent's behalf, witnessing that Ms. Gibby's appearance on Sabbath morning, or any other time, "testified to the Lord's presence as we gathered to pray."

One parishioner called her Mount Olive's "little light." Her reference to a gospel song I remembered singing as a child.

At which point the keyboardist sounded its first bar, as nearly everyone in the audience commenced waving their arms high and singing:

This little light of mine
I'm going to let it shine
Oh, this little light of mine
I'm going to let it shine
Hide it under a bushel? No!
I'm going to let it shine
Hide it under a bushel? No! I'm going to let it shine
Let it shine, all the time, let it shine.

Only then did I understand Ms. Gibby was Mount Olive's adult heart-innocent child.

> *But Jesus said, Suffer little children, and forbid them not, to come to me: for of such is the kingdom of heaven.[xii]*

When the service ended, a lady sitting alongside asked, "How did you make her acquaintance?"

I explained how she had become a major part of my life over the past couple months.

Then as if out of nowhere, the parishioner inquired if I knew Onkel Jakob. She broke into a wide smile. "Ms. Gibby left a space for him to sit alongside her where she always sat in the first pew. Said that he was her "man friend who needed to come to church bein' who he was outside it.""

"I know who he is," I replied. "He wore dancing cleats on his shoes."

The woman guffawed. "Oh Lord, yes! On some rousing Sabbath gospels we could hear his drumming time under Ms. Gibby's bottom."

Esther, heading up the aisle to leave, appeared surprised when she eyed me and my neighbor laughing.

But didn't linger.

On the sidewalk outside Mount Olive, Fern—bathed in the amber glow of a streetlight—signaled me.

Surprised, as I had already decided earlier that I would leave on my own. I'd deposited my belongings on Alsada's porch to be gathered after Gibby's remembrance. I hesitated in moving toward her, anticipating her barbed animus for not meeting in the dormitory. Fern gestured impatiently for me to hurry while displaying the hatbox containing Hannah's items.

"What? You think I don't know you well enough to find you here? Gibby fix her voodoo spell on you till the very end?"

We gathered our belongings and headed out of Blacktown.

No conversation between us.

After we had covered several blocks, Fern angrily swung around: "Shake a damn leg, Onkel Jakob! Ain't no time for dawdlin'."

CHAPTER NINE

Nobody dies. We know that.
  Oh, we profess they do and grieve at length because of it.
  Yet they squirrel their way back . . . on their terms.

Ichabod elegiacally professed that Hannah—or Bernadette, her preferred name—gave birth to me in Portsmouth on the banks of the Ohio River, then drowned herself at its and the Mississippi's confluence in Little Egypt. Her white kerchief head covering lingering on the water's surface like a Christ lily.

I'm indebted to Ernest for framing her death in that manner.

Except I've been given no choice as to when she appears before me or in what guise. Same for Onkel Jakob Bojangles.

The dead resurrect themselves within us.

Fern and I running off together like pubescent lovers? The subliminal baggage that each of us bore mocked our endeavor. Yet, for several days we acted out the fantasy inscribed in our libidos. My own was manifestly different than hers. For me her body was now mine in a way, an intangible in my imagination for too long, an inviolable reality of white heat and perspiration that I could explore with no inhibitions. I would lie next to her and witness her breast nipples gorge before my very eyes as I raced my fingers across them. And her black forest nether area that caused my groin to impulsively erupt by its very notion. How that place of origin with its own secret spring bathed my lips and tongue. Oh Jesus, I'd never experienced such delirium alongside this girl-woman.

And when my body began to shudder as never before, my loins a bonfire, all without entering her, I knew I had not yet metamorphosed into a man.

She lay alongside wearing a strained expression of condolence.

Yet betrayed by the flashing neon motel light outside our window, a Berea boy's spill of white seed limned her black thigh.

I reached down and pulled the quilt over my body.

Fern turned her back to me.

In the dusky armory's far corner, a glint of skylight illuminated Billy Coombs like he was clinging to the yard of a mast, the whirling Ichabod. An Albert Ryder vessel caught in a summer tempest, a young boy's maelstrom—mine—watching his father man-circling toward nightfall.

* * *

As we sat across from each other in a diner the next morning, Fern did her best to make light of what had occurred in bed the evening before.

Except I was unable to.

The pulsing red, green, and yellow neon sign lights had lit my alabaster self up like a circus display. As if they had paraded me outside a tent to advertise every vernal boy's sexual fantasy to be unveiled inside by women as old as their mothers.

The message I believed Fern had been conveying to me since we met.

"No such tents in Blacktown," I thought.

But shortly by noon we were on another bus heading east. We hadn't decided where to stop. She preferred the seat closest to the window and continued to point out sights that I'd no longer taken any notice of.

"Jeremiah! Look at that."

A cat sunning in barbershop window. A woman in an orange dress crossing herself. Grade-school girls leaping over sidewalk cracks.

That day we rode clear to Springfield, Missouri, before getting off at dusk. For the last several miles I had become apprehensive about our evening's plans. Fern had already taken charge. "Tonight *I'll* sleep by the window," she kidded. We took food up the steps of hotel, advertising "Rooms To Let Nightly." The black attendant greeted her and me like blood relatives.

"Nobody ever bother you here," he assured.

Fern paid him in bills out of the change-purse she pulled out of her blouse.

The room had purple walls and looked out on an alleyway below. An ashen light lay limp on the stained bedspread. One forlorn over-stuffed maroon chair sat alongside. She switched on the Bakelite radio and began dialing for music, all the while eyeing me.

"Look, Jeremiah. Leave it behind you . . . whatever it is gloomin' your damn head."

Fern pointed to the chair. "Ain't a soul that I can see sittin' there. Gibby, Onkel Jakob, or your damn Whitebread Berea brother who left me waitin' in the station.

"Gonna be different tonight."

After we dined on hunks of bread and cheese, starlight erased the memories of earlier tenants that graced the room's windowsill like dead flies. Fern pulled down the bedspread and motioned that I undress. Moments later she returned nude from the bathroom and crawled into bed alongside me.

"So relax," she comforted once again, hovering over me while with an index finger wrote her name upon my chest.

Then it returned, a passage that had long haunted me upon reading *Cane* in Alsada's boardinghouse dormitory:

> *I should have taken her in my arms the minute we were stowed in that old lifeboat. I dallied, dreaming. She took me in hers. And I could feel by the touch of it that it wasn't a man-to-woman love. It made me restless. I felt chagrined. I didn't know what it was, but I did know that I couldn't handle it. She ran her fingers through my hair and kissed my forehead. I itched to break through her tenderness to passion. I wanted her to take me in her arms as I knew she had that college feller. I wanted her to love me passionately as she did him. I gave her one burning kiss. Then she laid me in her lap as if I were a child. Helpless. I got sore when she started to hum a lullaby. She wouldn't let me go. I talked. I knew damned well that I could beat her at that. Her eyes were soft and misty, the curves of her lips were wistful, and her smile seemed indulgent of the irrelevance of my remarks. I gave up at last and let her love me, silently, in her own way.*[xiii]

The moon was non-existent this night. The air in our room musty, and every now and then, a sour tang drifted up from the alleyway. Fern had read these very words.

As I lay awaiting sleep in Springfield, it was as if Toomer had inscribed our hearts with his pen. That we had become his unwitting parchment. Each of us cast onto a page for eternity. That we were old now and performing out of ridicule for the benefit of a voyeur in an adjacent room.

I got up and looked outside the window.

A woman in an orange dress stared vacantly back at ours.

At daybreak Fern, fully dressed, occupied the chair that Onkel Jakob had sat in overnight. She was waiting to say something to me when I awakened. But I hadn't been asleep for hours. I simply lay there with my eyes closed, imagining her every movement. Metal garbage containers were being emptied into a refuse truck below. Daybreak music. Ours, however, breathed a forlorn air.

No words.

"Do you have enough money to get where you want to go?" she asked gently.

I nodded that I did.

"Did you notice the white rose on my breast last night? I put it there especially for you. They grow in Blacktown too." Fern stood and warmly embraced me. Then asked: "How far away is that place you and I were headed?"

I shook my head.

"'Cause I want to meet you there one day where Black girls are petals of dusk, the Gibbys don't ever perish, and white boys grow in the dark."

She took my hand and held it over her heart.

"Don't forget me, Jeremiah," she whispered. "I will never you."

From outside the hotel I watched her vanish down the street.

Not once did she look back.

I can't recall any other time in my life where I longed to be erased. A craven boy who had climbed too high in a Blacktown tree. And now I didn't care to be rescued. Even a feral cat skyward in an old oak deserved more.

Wandering aimlessly up, down, across the Springfield streets until dark did nothing to restore my wish to stay alive. Once the amber streetlights came on, the first tangible thought began to form, unaided by my consciousness. That's when I began to laugh out loud.

"You talkin' to me, Onkel Jakob?" I cried.

He didn't answer.

Instead I recalled Gibby's invite:

O-go-doe, Child, Mama's callin' you. Come along with me and Onkel Jakob. We're meetin' Hannah in Little Egypt where the mighty Ohio weds the Mississippi. O-go-doe, you can ride on the pale white Horse of Death on Halleluyah Street.

Her words evinced a clarity that I was familiar with. The pale white horse didn't frighten me. My mama existed in my head together with most of the other folks I'd encountered thus far in my life. Billy Coombs, Onkel Jakob, Ichabod, Chester Grange, Eva . . . and now Gibby.

But Alsada's boarding house enabled me to step outside of my head. My several-week stay there had liberated me from being captive to those characters largely of my own making. It was a sanctuary where the unexpected didn't exist.

Any surprise I reflected on had been already dated. Reason had tediously inscribed its narrative in my consciousness.

I had climbed into a dormitory bed with Esther and Fern.

At that moment I felt as if a birthing nurse had slapped me conscious, and I tasted the sweetness of breath for the first time. The rapture of lying alongside someone else sucking wind . . . instead of imagining my fabled mother mounted on the pale Horse of Death suckling me alive.

Oh, the images at times were more vibrant than mythical jewels.

Yet my grasping the hands of the twins that night in the dormitory felt like Hannah had finally arched me out of her womb . . . and I bawled like the baby I veritably was.

Sometime around midnight I found myself back at the hotel where Fern and I had stayed.

The genial manager I suspected had begun drinking as an aid to get through to daybreak. He wore a wide grin as he looked me over. "Where's the lady?" he inquired, like he already knew.

"Don't know," I said.

"I think I do."

I wished to believe him at first, but knew better.

"Each couple who come in here looking for a room, be it for an hour or a whole night, totes a story along with them. You know what I mean? What's your name?"

"Jeremiah."

"Oh Lord, yours go back to King David!" He chortled and set a fifth of bourbon on his desk, along with two shot glasses and poured.

"Oblige me, Jeremiah." It was my first taste of liquor.

We sat down in his cramped office.

I began feeling like I was back in the company of Ichabod.

"What was *our* story?" I asked.

"The Black young lady treatin' you like baby Jesus."

He sternly eyed me for a recognition.

"Ain't it so, right? I see how whipped you be."

He poured me another jigger.

"She be lookin' for a man to make her sing . . . instead she be hummin' a gospel to you. If you ask me, I'd say you were set up."

"I don't understand."

"Maybe she was jes' teachin' you a lesson, whiteboy. I don't mean no disrespect. Except that's the story I read once she paid me the bread.

"Meanwhile you believin' in your heart and stones you be the man."

He reached out his hand to me. "I am Lionel Gooding, Jeremiah." We shook.

I sat there nodding my head, muttering "Yeah, I be the man."

"Not for her, son. Some dude 'who longs to ripen a growing thing too soon' what she be lookin' for."

Now I knew Lionel and I had something in common.

"Jean Toomer," I muttered.

"It's how I dress up the stories come waltzin' in here. Otherwise they be boring me to death."

Lionel and I had become friends for life. Mine especially this dark night of the soul. The man had talked me out of racing to meet Ms. Gibby and Hannah on the pale gray steed of death. So close I could hear its hooves pounding impatiently on the sidewalk outside the hotel.

He handed me the keys to the room Fern and I shared.

"Go purge it of your bad memories, Jeremiah. Ain't no baby Jesus in that old bed that's experienced more comin 'n goin' since the immaculate conception. Which, by the way, is a bad word in these quarters.

"I'll talk to you in the mornin'."

I climbed the steps to the third floor and guardedly opened the door to our room, dreading I'd see her lying on the bed waiting for me.

Instead a full moon shined in off the alleyway window like an indigent at rest.

Except who was I kidding? Fern saw the glass wall.

The one separating me from others.

Even my new friend Lionel instinctively knew.

It's all that Ichabod was about . . . our many encounters.

Gibby had been living behind one too. Why else did she take up with Onkel Jakob? Like the alleyway moon in Lafayette Hotel's room No. 8 this night . . . we were all of a kind.

And as I lay there awaiting sleep, I wondered if Lionel might be one? He was an inveterate reader as was I.

"It's how I dress up the stories come waltzin' in here. Otherwise they be boring me to death."

I spotted Faulkner on his makeshift shelves along with Baldwin, Wright, Hurston, including poets Cullen and Hughes.

Every novel I read gifted me another means to breach the enclosure . . . if only for those times when I was relating to someone else on the other side. It's how I schooled myself in their manners, what they expected in exchange. When you are prisoner to the characters of your own creation, there is no mystery in the shared dialogue. And, sadly, often unrelenting . . .

Chatter. Chatter. Chatter.

As if there was anything of importance reciprocated.

For I have too often witnessed lone individuals talking to themselves on street corners . . . fearful that they were speaking to me or, say, Onkel Jakob. Overwhelmed by anguish passing one on the sidewalk, I'd fear the individual would nod recognition in a sideway glance.

Franz Kafka had a greater influence on me that my father ever did.

But one learns early on not to publicize such verity.

I looked about my room and at the empty chair, in a way surprised that Onkel Jakob was not there awaiting morning.

Instead my father had taken his place . . . sharing watching over me.

Was Onkel outside in the alleyway?

Billy's eyes were shut. Was he asleep or ruminating?

"Each time you looked at me, did you relive your shedding the brown habit off her body before assaulting her in the nave? Why else were you graced with a child while her cries were smothered in perpetuity?"

But Billy Coombs didn't dwell on such matters.

Otherwise I never would have encountered:

An Albert Ryder vessel caught in a summer tempest, a young boy's maelstrom—mine—watching his father man-circling toward nightfall.

All that I am able to recall from that night in No. 8 before falling asleep is Onkel Jakob tapping on Billy's shoulder to relieve him for a smoke.

By daybreak each had disappeared.

PART THREE

LAFAYETTE HOTEL

"The invisible has a mocking tendency to present itself as the visible . . ."

CHAPTER TEN

"The invisible has a mocking tendency to present itself as the visible, as if it might be distinguished from everything else, but only under certain circumstances, such as the clearing away of mist. Thus one is persuaded to treat it as the visible—and is immediately punished. But the illusion remains."[xiv]

A single knock on my door. Lionel stood there handing me a container of coffee. "Come downstairs once you are dressed and we'll talk." We sat facing each other in his cramped office. I was caught off guard before he even uttered a word.

Who are you? I thought.

I glanced at his bookshelves and wondered if he was a composite of the sundry characters he had absorbed in reading. How had he learned about women like Fern . . . or whitebread boys like myself?

Are you a novel, Lionel? One that is writing itself this very moment?

"Jeremiah, I've a proposition for you. I could use some assistance around here running this hot-sheet hotel." I suppressed a laugh. "Well, we must call the Lafayette for what it is. Even the mayor does despite his monthly sojourns here under risible disguise accompanied by one of his young male assistants.

"But that's another tedious story. Look, I'd like you to help me managing this place. Meeting the guests and helping me clean and make up the rooms they foul. Thankfully our clientele never expect much except privacy and a bed. In return for your assistance, there is always an empty room where you can sleep. Never the same one, unfortunately, but one you don't have to pay for. Also, several of our guests, especially the regulars like *hiz* honor, tip. If you are on duty, the gratuities are yours. That way you will never be without spending money.

"And finally, I could use the company being that it appears we share some things in common."

"What's that?" I asked.

"Your taste in women."

Lionel knew how to prick my naivete without leaving a scar. I loved that about the man.

"Offer accepted. Where do I begin?" He reached out to shake my hand. Inside his was a fresh twenty-dollar bill.

"Your first gratuity, Jeremiah. Enjoy an honest dinner on me tonight."

* * *

As if we owned it, for five consecutive weeks Lionel and I shared running the Lafayette. He never told me who did, but it didn't matter because he and I had become brothers despite our skin colors. Like Ichabod, a couple times each week he would return from the Springfield library with an armful of books, mostly fiction not of the page-turner genre.

I now had a room to sleep in whose number changed nightly. Lionel loaned me a white shirt and tie that I wore when managing the desk. When cleaning the rooms it was his preference that we wear a bandanna covering our heads and a clean white butcher's apron. Ostensibly it was to masquerade as hired help.

"Don't exchange glances with our guests if you happen to confront them while cleaning the rooms. That way they will never be certain if the management is checking their beds." He'd snicker.

Except I never knew for certain: *Was I one of the characters in the novel he was scribbling in real time?* More so, had I breached the glass wall by accepting Lionel's offer . . . or had each of us conspired to entertain ourselves at the expense of the other? Yet each of those weeks I worked at the Lafayette were the happiest I'd experienced thus far.

My mother's convent belongings I kept secreted in a backpack.

Gibby and Onkel Jakob ceased visiting me unexpectedly. Oh, they were still around, but now there was more going on outside their influence. Like who would come in off the street after dark at the Lafayette while I was on duty. And what current author I was reading would I reference to adorn the guests' hackneyed tale.

All the while, I let Lionel know how grateful I was to him.

"For finding your place in Springfield, Missouri! Christ, Jeremiah, I hope to hell that's not what you are saying." He was visibly distressed.

"I don't feel like running off as I did in Berea. That's all."

"Well, okay. But don't you begin fallin' for a damn story you are composing for yourself. I simply offered you a job for a short duration . . . nothing more, nothing less. A loan of my shirt and fucking red tie. Jeremiah, I got enough damn ghosts in my closet."

Lionel slapped his desk and walked out in a huff.

It was but a week later—my final stay at the Lafayette—when on a Wednesday past midnight, I had fallen asleep while manning the admittance desk and was startled awake by someone tapping the silver bell. Still hazy I withdrew the register from the office drawer when I eyed the guests.

Lionel stood there staring at me. Fern behind him, wearing a discomforting grin.

"No. 8 if you please, sir. We've been here before."

Initially, I assumed he was pranking me. That the two of them had worked it out as a harmless jest when they happened to run into each other earlier in the evening.

Except the couple wasn't the invisible presenting itself as the visible.

Lionel held his hand out, gesturing for the key. I slid it across Lafayette's counter to him. Fern had already begun to climb the three stories to their room. Undoubtedly it was author Lionel Gooding's introduction to his novel's Chapter Twelve that I had just experienced, leaving me crestfallen.

Thus one is persuaded to treat it as the visible—and is immediately punished.

Unable to bear the book's ending, I shed Lionel's shirt and red tie, depositing them on the desk with Lafayette's management keys alongside.

Once outside, I began walking to nowhere.

It all made sense. It was his work from the very start of allaying my shame for being a Berea white boy. Perhaps he was continuing to mentor me. And as an aside, I thought Fern looked a bit older and, if anything, more worldly wise, given that she made no discernible effort to explain what was taking place before my eyes. Her black heels announced each step she took to their room whereas her Chuck Taylors hadn't to our No. 8.

If I were writing his story, why shouldn't her pairing occur with someone like Lionel—a person I truly admired and liked—instead of a total stranger?

But why not just sack me, Lionel? I wondered.

Was it to prove to me that watching her ascend those steps wouldn't devastate me as much as I thought it would?

That your having done it with her hurt more . . . much more?

* * *

Yet peering into the Lafayette's window the next morning, I was struck to see Fern manning the desk. Her hair was pulled back into a tight bun, and she was wearing Lionel's shirt and tie. *For chrissake he's given her my job! Wasn't it sufficient what had already occurred between them the hours before?* However, glancing into the hotel's interior once more, Lionel stood there studying the desk register. No sign of Fern. The white shirt and red tie was his.

"It was all a misunderstanding" I tried to explain later. "Once I saw the two of you come in together . . ."

"What two of us?"

"You don't owe me an explanation, Lionel."

"For fucking what, Jeremiah?"

"I watched her go up the steps before you. No. 8, third floor."

He stared at me. "No. 8 has been occupied for several days now. You were the one who checked him in. Or don't you remember?"

It was after dark when the guest approached the desk. He smiled as if we had known each other at some point in our pasts. Each of us was unable to mask our embarrassment for not recalling when or how. He wore a rumpled Dobbs hat I suspected to hide a bald spot. I glanced down and noticed that his brogues held a glassy shine and wondered if he had joined joined Ichabod and Billy Coombs on the cavernous Ukrainian Hall dance floor years earlier.

Lionel firmly deposited the extra set of Lafayette's keys in my palm. "No. 12 is vacant. Get some sleep. We'll break out the bourbon later." When I turned to leave, he grabbed my shoulder. "The *Other* in you, Jeremiah, will write your story if you let it. Appears that's what been taking place in your damn head. I ain't been that lucky to betray you by bedding the lovely you waltzed in here with weeks earlier. Sadly, you 'n me are condemned to purloin our lives from scribblers. It's a tormenting condition . . . but consider the alternative."

The morning sun illuminated No. 12 that had been painted a cheery daffodil yellow. The color of a hat that I thought would look good on me . . . or Onkel Jakob, even.

As I lay there on the bed gazing at the ceiling, I couldn't swear that what I'd feared occurred between the two hadn't.

There is always a dance floor in somebody's past.

* * *

One day later, the vaguely familiar guest in No. 8 handed me a sealed envelope with the penciled letters J.C. "I found this under the bed this morning. Didn't know whether it was something of importance that another guest had left behind. Just in case, thought I'd leave it at the desk."

I thanked him. Once he was out of sight, I opened it, believing I recognized the handwriting and to whom it was intended. Inside was Hannah's Star of David cloth patch. My mind began racing.

There had been nothing left under the bed in No. 8 because I purposely looked there the day after Fern left, hoping she had left a piece of clothing, some item that captured her scent. Nothing but carpet lint.

Desire is the unknown—and it is the unknown that reigns.[xv]

The initialed envelope and what it contained burned hotter in my consciousness than the night our bodies chastely mingled in Alsada's dormitory. Then my desire for her came unannounced . . . but gingerly. Now this incident provoked mayhem this side of the glass wall. More exciting to imagine what it all meant than learning it meant nothing.

Even Lionel didn't have to know.

CHAPTER ELEVEN

I never felt more psychically alive when an item from those depths— like the envelope and Star of David—breached the veneer of reality that I could touch or smell. A hand, not mine, had inscribed my initials on that craft paper flotsam.

Oh-go-doe, Lord. Oh-go-doe. I'm returnin' home.

Gibby's cry of rejoice peeled like the bells of St. Andrews on Sunday morning. Someone *genuine and authentic; not artificial or spurious* had reached out to me.

"What's gotten into you?" Lionel inquired. "Something you haven't shared with me?"

I laughed his insinuation off. "What could possibly be going on here at the Lafayette that you aren't privy to?" I said. Not wanting to engage, he returned to entering the last week's receipts into the voluminous black leather accounts ledger.

I was loath to let Lionel in on the narratives I deliriously imagined the envelope might possibly birth. For it was now apparent to me that he *was* writing a book. Who is to say that he wouldn't steal the one emerging in my head? I'm convinced he felt a similar paranoia about me. There were moments when I even fantasized that we indeed were the sole custodians of the Lafayette Hotel whose outside placard read: "*Hospitality is not our custom here. We have no need for guests.*"[xvii]

Following an entire night after the stranger in No. 8 had handed me what I believed was Fern's initialed gift to me, I had now convinced myself that she was living there. That the envelope hadn't been left behind when Lionel and she had ostensibly enjoyed a one-nighter.

Why else had the man seldom left his room? Why did we look so familiar to each other? And most convincing of all . . . were the two pairs of shoes I'd spied under their bed.

Outfitted in the head bandanna and white butcher's apron, I knocked on No. 8's door, offering to clean it. He had barely opened it before muttering "No" . . . then banging it shut, but not before I spotted the Chuck Taylors alongside a black pair of women's heels.

Each floor of the Lafayette had three rooms, all with a bed, one overstuffed chair, and a lamp. It had been built in the early 1900s by a retired lobsterman from Maine who dressed the beds with quilts illustrating sea-and-ship motifs, supplied genuine clam shells as ashtrays, and attached room keys to miniature hand-carved buoys. "Why in Springfield, Missouri, God only knows," Lionel shrugged. "Guests kept clipping them. He soon replaced everything with the sleazy crap we use now."

A common bathroom lay at the far end of each floor. Sink, toilet, and a black-splotched bathtub missing ass-bottom patches of porcelain. No shower of course, commensurate with hot-sheet enterprises across the South.

I often hid there, thinking I might catch sight of Fern walking the hallway. Even stood out in the alleyway to peer into room No. 8's window, hoping to see her glancing back.

My best prospect I believed was catching her by surprise in the middle of the night. Unlike Esther who was the sedentary twin, she was always on the go. Three successive midnights I stood waiting in the stairway for her to wander outside and onto the street.

I longed to hear her voice again. Missed listening to her after dark in the dormitory reciting lines she'd memorized from *Their Eyes Were Watching God*. Most of all I wanted to inhale her sandalwood sudor once again. How it eddied at the base of her neck . . . beads of drizzle runneling across a moonlit alleyway.

Christ, Fern . . . you made my heart sing.

* * *

To my all-encompassing surprise, the guest in No. 8 appeared before me at the admitting desk one morning, gleefully slapping the silver summoning bell. "Jeremiah Coombs! What's a Berea boy doing way down here in Southland?"

"Who are you?" I asked, cold to his patronizing euphoria.

"On that bus with you, Billy, and Ernie 'Ichabod' Tyner to that infamous Kiner game in Pittsburgh a while back. Remember?"

"Sorry, but I don't recognize you."

"Oh, I wouldn't expect you to," hesitating like he was holding something back. "You look a lot like your mother, son."

"You knew her?"

"Before I worked alongside your father at the pottery. Yes." He abruptly cut our exchange short. "My name's there on your register.

It's as good as any if you want to talk."He took two steps at a time heading back upstairs.

The next morning under Lionel's watch, "Gregory Munson" checked out. I personally scoured the room and discovered not even a scintilla of evidence that Fern had ever been its occupant. Her earthy scent didn't linger in the bed linens. Nor even in the single limp bath towel at the end of their floor.

But something had changed.

Just as I had experienced the jubilation of breaching the glass wall when Munson handed my the envelope inscribed with my initials . . . within one week of his departure, Lionel handed me a letter addressed to *"J. Coombs, C/O Lafayette Hotel, Springfield, Missouri."* Vindication that I was alive to other than Onkel Jakob, *Oh go doe* Gibby, or even Hannah on her pale gray steed of death.

Further, this envelope veiled a lost voice inside.

> Jeremiah,
> I hope I've finally located you. I will only know if you write back.
> Otherwise, dear friend, I will keep looking.
> Our street in Berea is lost without you. Daily I pass your old house and
> hesitate, believing you might suddenly appear.
> So, reliving the times you did, I linger.
> Ernie Tyner
> PS: Gotta hold God tight. He tends to slide down your legs.

Munson had to be the source of my whereabouts. At Ichabod's instructions, he'd arrived at the Lafayette for the express purpose of learning more about me after leaving Berea. Also, I believe he had even visited Hannah's former convent. Otherwise, what provoked him to say "You look a lot like your mother" prior to taking flight before dawn the next morning?

As to how my old neighbor and friend knew to deploy an acquaintance to Springfield? The Sisters of Conscience, responding to his inquiry as Bernadette's sibling, shared what they knew about my mother's last days. Surely that connection led to Ichabod's learning of my presence at Alsada's boarding house.

Had Hannah and he secretly met following her encounter with Billy Coombs in St. Andrews darkened chancel, when she asked Ichabod to look after me?

If so, it meant she was still alive.

As was Billy Coombs, of course.

CHAPTER TWELVE

"The missive was in the hand of a former friend or relative from your home in Berea?"

"Yes."

"So, you have been found. Isn't that just wonderful?" Lionel's sarcasm bled into a contemptuous upbraiding.

"Why do you and I flourish here? It's because we've been emancipated by the pedestrian stories who sign our guest register each and every day. Do you possess a suicidal wish to relinquish all that the Lafayette affords us by consigning the rights of your story to the anonymous inscribed in that black leather graveyard of signatures?

"What are you afraid of, Jeremiah?

"Abandoning the plots you have already cribbed off our bookshelves to seek an identity? Are you that fragile? Haven't you already become aware how dangerous everyday life is? "

"My pen has disappearing ink, Lionel. The pages of a day's work often vanish overnight."

"Look, we are the custodians of Jehovah's choir who sing off-key before falling into a dead sleep. Parish bells with their clappers ripped out. Their cries of orgasmic release reverberate unanswered in our hallways.

"If you wish to avoid madness, Jeremiah, never stray far from your desk."[15]

That night in an untenanted room I dreamed that Onkel Jakob, outfitted in a Gestapo uniform, had plucked my tongue and placed it in a tiny crystal bowl which he sat on the kitchen window sill.

"Watch it sprout, son."

We were staying in Billy's and my Berea house. And for what seemed days, I sat their waiting for it to say something. But all I heard were the voices of others in the room: Billy's, Chester's, Eva's, Gibby's, even Fern's. My tongue thrashed about in vain attempting to answer. The house was alive with chatter.

I walked up the stairs to witness Jakob hang his uniform in an armoire whose doors were illustrated with refulgent white roses. Immediately I was overcome by deep sadness. The tongue lay wilting in the afternoon sunlight. Shortly, he would toss it out into the backyard, lamenting "Fucking Germans who lack green thumbs."

And we both laughed, except I no longer could.

Awaking in a sweat, I perceived my dream as echoing Lionel's exhortation:

"If you wish to avoid madness, Jeremiah, never stray far from your desk."

Yet in a crystal bowl my tongue appeared on the windowsill of every room in the Lafayette I cleaned that morning.

Onkel Jakob changed its water daily.

* * *

Could this be the reason for Ichabod's letter?

> *I hope I've finally located you. I will only know if you write back. Otherwise, dear friend, I will keep looking.*

---

15 *"If you wish to avoid madness, never stray far from your desk."* F. Kafka, *Letters to Friends, Family & Editors*, Schocken Books

Our street in Berea is lost without you. Daily I pass your old house and hesitate, believing you might suddenly appear.

To do what? Kill my father?

What better story for living, I thought. Given that it was he, Billy, who wrote its beginning lines inside her. *His offspring who would one day discover a reason for living?* The gift of a numbered room that was certifiably my own? Why else had I visited Little Egypt except to seek Hannah out? For she had carried me there where the Ohio and the Mississippi converge.

How does one write their story when its already been written? Was I doing anything other than following its plot lines? The Sisters of Conscience and Alsada's boardinghouse preceded my birth. It was Gibby who revealed what Hannah had confided in her prior to walking into *The Gathering of Waters*.

Whereas I, the respite for the non-living. Onkel Jakob and Gibby lie alongside each other in my dormitory at night. His uniform and her wedding gown share a wooden hanger in my armoire.

* * *

The absurd irony of it all. When Lionel saw me with a pen poised over my notebook, he asked what I was writing. "A murder mystery," I replied.

"Oh?"

"Yes. It's come together in the past couple of days. I know both the perp and his victim. Now I discover how each navigates his fate."

"So, the monkey's off your back? Your addiction for cribbing plots to justify their vacancy in your own tissue of lies." He laughed.

"Let me put it this way, Lionel. She's no longer writing my story."

"Who?"

"*The petal of dusk.*"

Amused, he placed his hands together as if in prayer.

"She no longer inhabits the anonymous room I enter each night to sleep."

"God have mercy, Jeremiah."

"It's not to say that I don't miss her, you understand."

"Only too well, my friend."

Lionel's unsardonic response led me to infer that perhaps Fern's chimera presence in the Lafayette had become corporeal for each of us. The petal of dusk illuminating its hallways of impotence.

Now, as I lay awaiting sleep each night, I began scribbling the pages of the mystery in my head. What I found most intriguing was to what extent the victim had in writing his own story. *Having impregnated Hannah, had Billy Coombs effectively spawned the weapon that would kill him? During my boyhood years, were there acute moments when he would look at me and wonder how and when I might commit the act?*

Could he honestly have expected any other outcome? Holy water is not eyewash. The brown habit and the layers of cloth under it had been defiled. Her cincture knot untied. Inseminating a sister beneath the rood of Christ . . . a Berea eager fatalist's homily?

And as its scion grew more inward, wouldn't the dreams of his eventual fate bloom more graphic? Predestined acts often take root in sanctuaries.

The Sister of Conscience Incident refreshed St. Andrews's wearied liturgy.

In nómine Patris, et Fílii, et Spíritus Sancti. Dóminus vobíscum
Kýrie eléison Christe eléison Kýrie eléison

Had Billy Coombs already visualized our final hours together? Could that be the reason he and Ichabod began walking to the bus together each morning? Had Hannah's sacred and profane lovers found peace with each other as they circled toward nightfall?

Awaiting a son's mythic vengeance.

* * *

In me, my father's seed, resided his demise.

What other reason for my existence? I pondered in the days I remained at the Lafayette.

Billy Coombs surely viewed his fate in Hannah's eyes that night before slinking back into St. Andrews dark interior. She knew what she had been carrying inside her upon her return to the convent. *Jehovah's Vengeance.* That was rightfully my name. *Jeremiah* a conceit suggested by Gibby perhaps. There was destined no bonding mother-son relationship between Hannah and me. She knew.

> *"Dearly beloved, avenge not yourselves, but rather give place unto wrath: for it is written, Vengeance is mine; I will repay, saith the Lord."*[16]

My father's fate had become mine.

God had slipped down our pantlegs.

* * *

The Lafayette Hotel . . . where your name bears no relevancy as to who you may be; where your room is never yours and everyday life is viewed as dangerous; where identities are cribbed from a graveyard of signatures, and doppelgängers cram its hallways lost.

It's there I lay alongside the petal of dusk, the memory of which lingers like a cardinal on my windowsill each dawn.

I will miss Lionel who perhaps was none other than myself befriending me.

He and I viewed greeting one another in the morning as a welcome affirmation of our actuality. The Lafayette's proprietor unlisted on its door or any other.

Anticipating my desire to leave covertly, Lionel had pinned a note to the guest register ledger the morning of my departure.

---

16 Romans 12:19: KJV

"Godspeed, friend. My wish is that one day you and I will meet to share what we have labored over while residing in Hotel Lafayette. It may surprise each of us."

Hannah's folded garments accompanied my meager belongings in the backpack.

PART FOUR

THE REUNION

"I hope I've finally located you. I will only know if you write back."

CHAPTER THIRTEEN

"Festivities sniff out disgrace. They unite communion and wound, marriage and immolation. They are the heirs of sacrifice."[xviii]

I arrived in Berea on the eve of All Saints' Day. Being that St. Andrews church was located next to the bakery at the bottom of our street, several makeshift carnival booths blocked it off for this occasion and the following All Souls' Day. So as not to be recognized, I witnessed the activity from the shadows of the alleyway that ran behind both structures. The children outfitted in masks and costumes their mothers had made to represent one of a hundred or more saints they had chosen at random from the church's Christmas calendar. It was an eve of levity, a uniquely rare occasion endorsed by the parish, given that mockery was the festivity's *raison d'etre*.

What better way to humanize Padres Thomas Fenn and Gerald Ricciardo than to honor the children by permitting their natural instincts? The carnival of costumes ranged from piercingly subtle to offensively gross. But no church police were in attendance. The Fathers mingled among the crowd and their good-natured laughs, I thought as adolescent, sounded not unlike what I expected to emanate from inside a bordello. In fact, I visualized the priests on this festive eve as stripping off their cassocks before the throngs and in return baring their naked bodies in jest. For many of us, we'd presumed the Fathers were pricks because they didn't have any.

Yet this All Saints' Day eve was different than all others I recalled. The adults in sundry masquerades had joined in the parish's saturnalia, except later following the time allotted for the children. The booths offered various midway games, contests, and delicacies for their pennies. Magdalena, the bakery owner, was dressed up as buxom blond Fräulein who had lost her voice and whistled her gestures. The line for her cream puffs trailed up Cascade Street far beyond Billy Coombs's domain. She dispensed them to eager palms like kisses.

The eve always had ended with a brief performance by the Blessed Bartolo Longo Orkestra, all brass instruments, comprised of parishioners, perhaps Berea's most favorite institution. Following a rousing rendition of "Goin' Up Yonder," the youngsters began to wander home sampling their treat bags while many of the adults commenced heading over to the grounds at the rear of the church.

In the past when the band sounded its last note, the day ended.

To my utter surprise the large grassy lot had been turned into a cemetery with numerous upright and horizontal headstones the color of salt licks and one ersatz mausoleum a tad larger than an outhouse. A bouquet of carnations and snapdragons decorated each marking while several baskets of salmon gladiolas adorned the perimeter of the mausoleum. In the center of the yard rose an elevated throne on which sat a replica of the Holy Father's Vatican chair but this one painted carmine red.

Unlike the children, the adults masqueraded as generic parish priests. Several boorish male parishioners exchanged traditional Roman soutanes for ones that looked more like skirts baring their hairy legs and blucher shoes. But mostly all alluded in some fashion to an effeminate predilection of the clergy. Say, a colorful silk handkerchiefs sprouting out of the cassock's arm, flowers adorning the clerical collar, or simply how someone walked about, gesturing in a dandified conceit. Also, there were more males in attendance than women whose costumes on the whole were more discreet, given that they didn't resort to mockery but instead to adoration.

Fathers Fenn and Ricciardo never looked so pious. Both priests stood alone and ceremonially erect at the rear of the church. An air of expectation soon quieted the revelers. Obviously an indication that everyone present, except possibly me, knew what was about to occur.

That's when I first laid eyes on Ichabod. "The Son of Jesus" in cloth tunic and sandals being led by the Fathers to the prelate's throne. Christ's crown of thorns supplanted by a crown of gold. A recognition for his years of never missing a Sunday Mass. St. Andrews's parish model of humility . . . cynosure of piety for all disciples of Jesus.

Following this brief ceremony, I sensed that the dozens of costumed adults skirting the mock gravestones and mausoleum were fraught with anticipation. They kept looking behind and around them, others trying to spy into the backyards surrounding St. Andrews's grassy lot. Then I began to observe that each of the stones had surnames on them, several familiar to me. Those of friends with whom I once attended school. Clearly the markers were clones of the actual ones located in one of the three Berea cemeteries.

I began to suspect that the costumed adults were the survivors of the deceased. *But what were they so anxiously looking about for?*

Only then did I witness a veritable storm of black-clad figures, masked by women's mourning hose cloaking their faces, rush pell-mell onto the make-believe dooryard of buried souls. Under the moonlit darkness they looked like stygian locusts, each furtively seeking the stone they wanted to chance.

For then I understood.

These were the spirits of the deceased returning for alms to carry them through the underworld until the succeeding All Saints' Day revelry.

In essence the occasion was not all that unlike the bingo games held each Thursday evening in the basement of St. Andrews. The actual identities of the returning spirits remained anonymous. They were parishioners randomly chosen. And being that several of the grave-stones represented this night bore the names of several prominent

Berea families, the alms dispensed could be quite generous. Each stygian locust prayed they had fallen onto one of the lucky graves.

It was only when a decedent's stone was approached by a living relative did the expectation reach its apogee. For there before them lay the returning spirit of, say, their father or mother, perhaps a beloved sibling, trembling in an uncontrollable paroxysm of grief, only assailed or satisfied by the amount of dollars rained upon the spirit's body.

That's when the whoops rose to the nightfall sky. The more generous descendants received the loudest huzzahs. Several spirits rose from their grief as if born again and circled the other less fortunate locusts triumphantly. While those who had chosen the stones of tight-fisted parishioners continued to lie on the ersatz markers weeping.

All the while the honored church member for the All Saints' Eve festivities, Ernest Ichabod Tyner, sat smiling in his bloodred throne none the wiser.

I presumed.

* * *

When only the custodians remained to clear the churchyard of the *in extremis* bouquets and sham gravestones—the mausoleum was actually the parish toolshed—I began walking up my former street. Undecided if I would return to Billy Coombs's house or continue on and knock on Ichabod's door, I spotted a light in my father's room. Having been away for several months, I couldn't tell if the lamp switched on automatically at dusk to give the illusion the house was occupied.

Was he still tight with Magdalena, the confectioner?

I chanced entering my former home through its back door. Once inside I called *"Hello?"* several times. No response. Walking through the kitchen and into the living room, it felt as nothing had changed since I'd left. Even the air felt dead. Not one thing in my upstairs bedroom had been touched it seemed. There was a thick layer of dust on my chest of drawers. Billy's room with its carefully made bed and secondhand woman's vanity he'd presumed might lend an air of familiarity to who he accompanied through its door on a Friday night. His theatrical set, so to speak, on which he prided himself for how well it seemed to persuade.

Never once had I seen him sit at the vanity or stare in its flaking silver mirror. I do know, however, he stored his "safes" in its right hand drawer.

As I lay in my bed that first night back in Berea, my memories of the house and Cascade Street cinematically played across the ceiling all in chiaroscuro. I had to keep reminding myself why I had returned, except the nostalgia for the past—despite having joyfully escaped it—lulled me into a deep sleep.

Only to be abruptly awakened by the overhead light and Billy standing at my bedside.

"What time is it?" I asked, trying to gather my bearings.

"Midnight. I spotted you at the festivities. Why didn't you tell me you were returning? I'm still your father, you know?"

He acted modestly peeved. Yet I sensed he was pleased to see me. One of those fond memories I had relived an hour or so earlier was the time he and I spent alone in the house, perhaps in separate rooms, finding comfort that neither of us were there alone. Almost always before heading off to bed we signed off with "See you in the morning."

Why that exchange solicits comfort in another human being, I'm not sure. Perhaps it was a deterrent for keeping the maw of existential loneliness at bay. The anguish of calling out in the night or early morning and there is no response.

At the very least he and I mutually embraced that reductive human conceit in common.

"Anyway, Son, I'm glad to see you back. I told Magdalena I'd be staying with you tonight. We'll talk in the morning."

Billy closed my door. Only when he was with a woman did he

ever shut his. I listened as he turned the bed covers down and removed his shoes.

Did he have any idea why I'd returned home?

* * *

He'd bought fresh coffee and pastry for our breakfast. As we sat down in the kitchen, I responded in generalities to his questions as to where I'd been and whom I'd met. Billy wasn't pleased with my response, brusquely pushing his chair away from the table. The irony was rich given he was the master of blank stares to my questions as a kid.

He lit a cigarette and tried again. "Do you plan on seein' Ernest?"

I nodded that I did.

"What did you think about the Fathers commemorating him last evening?"

"You mean *The Son of Jesus* tableau?" I laughed.

Billy shook his head. "Christ, what was all that about?"

"Beats me," I said. "What I watched in the churchyard caused me to think the St. Andrews priests were turning senile. Or then again maybe something nefarious was occurring before our very eyes."

"Whadaya mean?"

"Oh, I don't know. I was just thinking maybe they were making a spectacle out of our neighbor."

"You suggesting they were mocking him?"

"Yeah. Something like that. No Bible picture book I ever seen substituted a chintzy crown of gold for one of thorns. Also, what were they insinuating with the red papal chair?"

"Maybe you've been away from Berea too long, Jeremiah. Magdalena and I saw nothing malicious in the priests giving just due to Ernest's reflecting our better selves. Can't say the same for Billy Coombs."

"What about the headstone drama?" I asked.

He let out a loud chortle. "I've always believed that a jester and not the clergy should officiate the laying of bodies into the ground.

Jesus, wouldn't it make just as much sense to fly them to heaven on? Give me a damn break."

Billy got up and strode to the kitchen door where he turned eyeing me with a face-wide grin. "That girl you met on your trip south, Son. She plannin' on visitin' you here? If so, just let me know so our women don't mingle.

"It's your house too, right?"

Saint Ichabod and Billy Coombs, libertine: I was now certain the pair had been colluding.

* * *

"Festivities sniff out disgrace. They unite communion and wound, marriage and immolation. They are the heirs of sacrifice."

Alongside my father's double-breasted blue-serge suit, I hung Hannah's habit, veil, and cincture in his bedroom closet. Moments later,

I was not surprised to hear someone tapping on the kitchen door's glass. St. Augustine's "Son of Christ" caricature stood outside. I was unable to separate the Ichabod I had known and loved with the All Saints' Eve commemorated Ernest Tyner of a night before. He, too, wore a tentative expression when we greeted each other.

"Come in, please." I assisted in removing his jacket. "Oh, it's so good seeing you again."

Ichabod embraced me, then held me at arm's length.

"Jeremiah, you've grown. I mean to say you are no longer that young man I bid goodbye to nearly a year ago. Welcome home, dear friend."

What was my expression revealing on its own volition?

We sat across from each other in Billy's living room. "I'm on my way to the pottery, so I can't stay long. But I just had to see you, son."

I was uncertain if I should tell Ichabod I'd seen him earlier. Except he appeared to anticipate my quandary.

"Did Billy fill you in on the parish's churchyard festivities last night?" With a self-deprecating air, he spread his arms widely. "*'Church Fathers Honor Ernest Tyner.'* You will read it in tomorrow's paper."

"With a crown of gold," I muttered.

"Oh, you were among the crowd. Yes, of course. *Recognition in the Churchyard.* For what, Jeremiah? *Jew of Cascade Street, Ernest Tyner, Makes Good.* I'm unable to read my brethren's heart."

Ichabod was loath to dismiss what had occurred to him on All Saints' Eve. He anguished the parish Fathers' intent. *Were they even capable of knowing?*

I'd implied as much as I dared. Unlike other St. Andrews' parishioners, as far as I was concerned Ichabod exemplified the teachings of Christ in a most unassuming and humble manner. One could only hope that his Irish and Italian neighbors hadn't unwittingly taken part in an Ecclesiastical Satire. At my mentor's urgings, I'd read the *Dubliners*. So, I know he had. Fathers Tom and Jerry felt unworthy of a Joycean clerical jab. But having grown up in the parish where each priest had served since my boyhood, despite my being a lack-luster St. Andrews' member, I was not innocent to the Vatican's neutrality during the Holocaust nor Pious XII's abject failure to identify Nazis as the evildoers. How could I not also imagine that these prosaic clergy were, in effect, perpetuating a dark medieval fantasy no stranger to Rome?

Festivities . . . the heirs of sacrifice.

My friend, acutely conscious to what I was thinking during these tense moments between us, had lowered his head. "I'm sorry you were there." He looked me in the eyes. "I wouldn't have attended if I'd known you'd be among the revelers. Yes. Fathers Fenn and Ricciardo, dare I say, were pimping for the avowed anti-Semites in the crowd. With priestly self-regard they hiked their chasubles to pleasure the haters while officiating as servants of the Lord.

"They purchased me for a crepe paper crown of gold, Jeremiah."

Ernest grabbed his jacket and left. I watched him walk disconsolately to the bus stop.

On my way to the grocery store that afternoon, I witnessed the church custodians using steel wool and paint remover to strip the Presider's Chair of its incarnadine hue.

* * *

In the days following, except for a trip to the grocery store, I stayed in Billy's house. Yes, it asserted that it was still mine too, but I had no intention of staying once what I had returned to Berea for was accomplished. I neither saw him nor spoke to Ichabod as he passed by twice daily on his way to and from the pottery mill. I presume my father and he continued to meet on the bus, given that Magdalena's place was only one street over from ours.

A good portion of my waking hours was preoccupied by one question: *After relinquishing her identity as Hannah and fulfilling the years long Sisters of Conscience novitiate training, why had Bernadette returned to Berea?*

Or for whom?

Ichabod's watching out for me—his mentoring—had not

occurred by happenstance. Nor did the strange companionship he and Billy Coombs ostensibly shared. I'd come to that conclusion much earlier. But what did either have to do with my mother's death?

The first nights I spent alone in the house, I envisioned Bernadette wandering anguished through its rooms. The fingers of her right hand repeatedly caressing the rope cincture's four knots: her vows of chastity, poverty, obedience, and enclosure.

Why had she returned to this place where as an infant I'd last seen her?

But unlike then, we did not visit. I'd await her nightly presence in my doorway in vain. There were no reassuring footsteps on the stairway outside. I never saw her face.

> *Mother, you are elusive as God. Permit me to feel the breath your brown habit stirs as you flurry past.*
> *Even the silver Crucifix suspended above my bed is void of reflection.*
> *At your watery grave did you utter my name?*
> *Void of words, I bawled yours at birth,*
> *The red scapular sweeping newly fallen snow in our path.*

Who or what caused Bernadette to threaten her vow of enclosure? Did she covertly leave the convent or request permission from its Abbess? Either way, given her veneration, the averred reason compelling that she return briefly to Berea I'd come to suspect was a fabrication.

My mother took her own life as Hannah, not Sister Bernadette, because of Billy Coombs or Ernest Ichabod Tyner. Why, I am not sure. Nevertheless, the mighty Ohio flows into the Mississippi. She followed it home.

* * *

Each man was purposely keeping his distance from me. When Ichabod strode up Cascade Street after work, I'd watch from the living room window to see if he'd surreptitiously glance at our house. He never did. Also, my occasional visits to the bakery yielded little more than cream puffs and innocuous greetings from Magdalena, masquerading what actually was on my father's mind.

This was not how I intended the story to evolve, I thought. *They were my chosen characters, except I had metamorphosed into their principle one whose plot had paradoxically brought Ichabod and Billy closer.*

I'd not returned to Berea to become victim of its proneness to innuendo, rumor, and paranoia like the parishioners of St. Andrews who had capitulated to the dark trinity of whispers and delusions fostered by Fathers Fenn and Ricciardo.

Festivities unite communion and wound, marriage and immolation.

The churchyard's All Saints Eve Alms Offering and Presider's Chair its veritable garden.

* * *

It had to be either Ichabod or Billy who first suggested to the other that I, Jeremiah, was plotting to avenge my mother's death, inasmuch that the notion hadn't even materialized prior to Ernest's seeking my whereabouts.

For how long had the anxiety stalked their waking hours?

Holed up in Billy's house, I could understand his paranoia. But that of my mentor I could only attribute to his commitment of keeping my best interests at heart. He knew what his dance partner was capable of doing.

Except, if that was true, why would Ichabod align himself on Billy's behalf?

What were they hiding from me?

Hoping Ichabod might change his mind and stop by to speak to me, I waited on the porch as he walked up our street on Friday at dusk, the close of his work week. I know he saw me. Except he eyed only the macadam walking by. I could barely resist calling out to him.

Later that evening when I was about to turn in and switched off all the lights in the house, I heard knocking on the backdoor. Believing it was Ernest, I opened it to confront Onkel Jakob flashing a sardonic grin. "You were expecting company, perhaps?" Behind him in the shadows stood Chester and Eva.

The three of them walked past me into the living room.

"Whadaya have to eat?" Onkel hollered.

"We're famished," Eva countered.

I could hardly make them out in the darkened room. Chester and she sat on the sofa and Onkel in his favorite overstuffed lounge chair by the front door. He had his feet up on its tufted ottoman.

"Kitchen's closed for the night. It's close to midnight," I replied. "If you want a drink, I can accommodate you."

Onkel gestured he did, and proceeded to help himself. Billy kept a rustic wooden box in the room to store kindling for the seldom used fireplace. Overtime it had become the liquor and shot glass cabinet. Chester and Eva passed when offered to join.

Onkel immediately broached the question: "Does Ichabod know why you are here?"

How could I prevaricate to a ghost? Especially one in my family? What was it that he didn't already know.

I joined Chester and Eva on the sofa.

"That's why he's pretending I haven't returned. He passes this house twice a day and never once has he glanced over. Except that first day when he knocked on my door. I imagine he merely wanted to see how much time he and Billy had before I would act. He was checking my temperature, so to speak."

"But he's your friend, Jeremiah," Chester replied. "I don't get his joining Billy Coombs. Ichabod, of all people, would have murdered Billy with his own hands if he'd bore witness to what occurred that night in St. Andrews's apse." Eva nodded.

I eyed Onkel Jakob. "I thought you might know."

"What makes you think that?"

"Billy's your son."

The old man laughed. "Yeah, and they dance together beautifully."

"Yet the Son of Christ isn't given to sleeping with women," I shot back.

"Even your mother?" Onkel parried.

I jumped up ready to attack him. But Chester pulled me back down into the sofa.

"You demonic German bastard!" I cried. "Your fucking son accosts her, and now you rape her once more in broken English. Have at it. Your day's long overdue."

"My day, son? That's rich. Come, sit on my lap and give old granddad a kiss."

Onkel Jakob returned to the wood box for a second round. I poured myself one. Chester gestured he was in this time.

By now only the amber streetlight's illuminating their eyes gave evidence of my visitors' presence.

For several minutes not one of us spoke. An ominous silence suddenly broken by footsteps on the front porch. I stood up and looked out the living room window.

Ichabod gestured for me to open the front door. None of my guests appeared surprised.

"Ernest, please come in," I said.

"Billy's coming up the street," he cautioned. "Please ask your friends to leave. I'll speak to you in the morning."

When I turned around, the living room looked like it always did . . . barren of visitors. As if it were a *tableau vivant* of an aged furniture store showroom. Ghostless.

I shut the front door and climbed the steps to my bedroom.

Moments later listening to the fractured rhythm of Billy's assent to his room, I knew he had spent Friday evening at the saloon on County Line Road.

For the first time in my life, I turned the key in my door's lock.

Vainly I listened to see if he did likewise.

CHAPTER FOURTEEN

Come daybreak I waited until Billy was dressed and out of the house before unlocking my bedroom door. Shortly after, Ichabod appeared on the porch, gesturing that I join him there. I poured each of us a cup of coffee and sat alongside.

"You might ask why I alerted you last evening to Billy's coming up the street?"

"Yes."

"Jeremiah, he's your father. Do you for a moment think he is any less capable of doing what you are apparently considering?"

"It's why I locked my bedroom door."

"But ponder who he believes is occupying his house."

"Except I've never said anything. You and Billy apparently have decided why I'm here."

"You've given us little choice, son."

"But it was you, friend, who sent Gregory Munson to the Lafayette Hotel in Springfield to spy on me. What was that all about?"

Ichabod stared out at the street for several moments before answering.

"Believe it or not . . . Billy Coombs's conscience."

We both laughed, he less heartily than me.

"Call it that if you so choose. I prefer to see it as abject fear. We will act out this charade of all's well . . . that is, until it no longer is."

Ichabod nodded gravely. "So, it *is* why you returned."

"What choice did I have? Why didn't Hannah drown us both?

As her son, how am I to interpret being left behind other than to avenge her death? That's what is driving his paranoia. And for good reason."

"Who strikes first?"

"Doesn't matter, does it? Father or Son."

Ichabod stood to leave. "I want you to promise me one thing: alert me first before you decide to act. I ask nothing more of you."

He walked back toward his house without awaiting my response.

The die had been cast. I was now my father's curse residing in his house that once also was mine. Whether Billy had spread the word among his saloon cronies, or not, I increasingly felt that I was being perceived a pariah in my neighborhood. At the grocery store and bakery, familiar faces keeping their distance from me had become the norm.

Frankly, their actions only confirmed why I had left Berea in the first place.

I'd not returned because of its susceptibility to the dark trinity of innuendo, rumor, and paranoia like the St. Andrews' parishioners who'd capitulated to the whispers and delusions fostered by Fathers Fenn and Ricciardo.

* * *

That very afternoon I received a letter from Lionel written on Hotel Lafayette stationery he once confided he'd reserved only for those guests who wished to pen suicide notes.

> *Dear Jeremiah,*
>
> *That mystery novel you are composing? Well, maybe this will add to it. I recently received a note from the lovelier-than-a-starlit-night woman you initially checked into the Lafayette with. (Apologies for resurrecting an especially mortifying memory, bro.) And for whatever godforsaken reason, she expresses interest in getting in contact with you.*

Women! I've told you what I think about her. But it's why we write, isn't it? No Yearning + No Ambiguity = No Story.

Enclosed is Fern's note and address.
In solidarity,
Lionel

* * *

Whitebread she wanted to speak to? But he's dead, Fern.

Jeremiah's *other* is currently focused on a more direct and unequivocal condition than boyhood impotency. I'm not so sure you and he would have much in common now.

Yet, you continue to haunt my dreams.

"I come back to tell you, brother, that white faces are petals of roses. That dark faces are petals of dusk."[xix]

I was not surprised to see Onkel Jakob show up that very night for no other reason, I believe, than to divert me from what I felt predestined to accomplish. He stood at the foot of my bed.

"Billy's ask me to intervene."

He was dead serious.

"Do you think he fears what you might do to him? That he is afraid of your taking his life?" Onkel laughed. "You fool yourself, boy. What has life given him except what's he's taken? No, he didn't lock his bedroom door like you did the other night. That's not what he was afraid of.

"His kind never are.

"How else does he know he's alive if it's not your presence? Haven't you asked yourself why he hasn't struck first? Think about it. Hasn't he always acted in self interest?

"You are at a greater risk of dying than he. *Don't you owe him some fealty?*"

Like Ichabod had earlier, Onkel Jakob didn't wait around for me to respond.

Nor was I surprised upon spotting a pair of Chuck Taylor's white tennis shoes at the side of my father's bed.

Onkel Jakob had surreptitiously placed them there.

And on the bottom step of the stairway to our bedrooms.

At the foot of the living room sofa like she had kicked them off while lying there speaking with me.

I even spotted them neatly paired in the bathroom, her glistening black body gracing its white porcelain tub.

> *I look forward to seeing you again, Fern. Let me know where and when.*
> *Jeremiah*

Except it was Ichabod who answered my response to her. He'd slipped a note under the living room door. "She is arriving by bus tomorrow. You and I will meet her at the Greyhound station downtown Berea at noon."

* * *

And how soon would he detect I was still smitten by the petal of dusk?

I first spotted her through the bus window. She was standing in line, waiting to get off, and wore a hat a bit understated than those the women wore at Gabby's church memorial. I'd known her when she would have placed it on her head as an innocuous slight of her elders. Except now it signified her authority as a self-aware woman of color.

Fern smiled and gestured to me upon stepping off the Greyhound, but headed directly for Ichabod like they'd enjoyed a long standing friendship. Dressed in an elegant black silk shantung skirt and jacket with Chinese knot enclosures, she embraced him warmly.

Embarrassed at my having to stand off to the side as a detached observer, he grasped the two of us together.

About to dance? I wondered.

Fern took a step away from me as if she were attempting to align her memory with the person who eyed her for answers.

"Jeremiah Coombs! Who would have guessed?"

Ichabod looked ill at ease.

"Gibby sends you her love." She winked at me, before turning to him.

"Once upon a time, me and him were brother and sister Oreo who resided in a story called *The Dormitory*. Gibby and Onkel Jakob, her discreet lover, were its narrators. We even slept alongside each other, didn't we, Jeremiah?"

"More than once," I replied.

Breaking out of her restrained self, she lustily chortled an opening, permitting Ichabod and me to join in.

We took a taxi to Cascade Street with me sitting next to the driver and Fern alongside Ernest in the backseat.

"Isn't there anything special about Berea you wish to point out?" she asked him, while glancing out the cab's window.

"What do you see?"

"Street after street of run-down houses looking like nobody's alive inside them."

"Exactly. Soon we will be driving up to Jeremiah's and mine"

Once inside his bungalow, after being shown the upstairs guest room and taking several minutes to unpack, she joined Ichabod and me in his living room.

He had poured her a cup of tea. "Chamomile, wasn't it?"

Fern grinned. "Thank you, Ernest."

So, you two have been together in the past, I thought. *What else should I know?*

In short order he dispensed with inquiring after Alsada and her father's well-being, before addressing who was really on his mind: Sister Bernadette.

The intensity of concentration Ichabod's body betrayed took me by surprise. *Had my deceased mother brought them together . . . and not me?*

Curiously, he began recalling what Hannah enjoyed eating. "Did Alsada ever serve roasted Brussels sprouts, Fern?"

"Only because Hannah enjoyed them so much."

"What about barbecued ribs?"

"You picturing how she lustily attacked them with her fingers?" Fern teased. "So out of character for a devout Sister's betrothed-to-Christ wedding ring be glazed with pork grease, correct?"

Ichabod wryly nodded. "That was the Berea in her."

For several moments no one spoke. It felt as if each of us was rifling our memories for moments with Hannah. Ichabod appeared mesmerized by his.

"Jeremiah, how did you and Ernest meet?"

"I watched him dancing with my father."

"Oh, Jesus!" Ichabod commenced to evoke the Ukrainian Hall coupling.

At its close, Fern turned to me: "Will I get to meet him?"

"Who?" I asked, partly in jest.

"The man who slides down God's pantleg."

"He'll give you no choice," Ichabod quipped. Quickly adding: "Fern, you probably haven't eaten anything since breakfast." He exited and momentarily returned with a tray of cheese selections and crackers. The latter provoked me to risibly erupt. I eyed Fern to see if her expression mirrored an uncomfortable memory we shared.

No satisfaction.

Her allegiance this hour belonged unmistakably to Ernest.

I'd have to bide my time until she and I were alone.

* * *

Upon showing up at Billy's house that night, "Why no photographs on the walls?" she queried.

"It's not that kind of home, Fern. Certainly not like Alsada's."

"Hannah's might be an exception, don't you think?"

"Except it's Billy house."

She tepidly nodded. "So, you must be curious why I'm here visiting your friend?"

"And not me?"

She laughed in a manner that immediately melted the barriers I'd erected to protect myself. Despite her "sophisticated lady" demeanor and fashion conceit, it was the feisty twin of Alsada's dormitory that sat a foot away from me. Not close enough to be bridled by her sandalwood bouquet, but perhaps too close if I was to remain alert.

"Yes, why Ichabod, Fern? Forget about me . . ." I stopped short of stating the obvious that she already had.

"Ostensibly it was you, Jeremiah, who prompted his visiting our house in Portsmouth. Alsada's warm feelings for you gave him easy entrance into our lives. I'd returned back home for a brief stay while Esther had gone off to college. Ernest came bearing gifts for each of us. Even for my father a lovely kente cloth shawl of cotton and silk. In fact, within a day or two of his living among us it was impossible not to recall our time when Hannah was an integral part of the family.

"And only then did we discover why he had come. It was for your mother."

She had taken me by surprise.

"For Hannah and not Sister Bernadette?"

"There was never any distinction. They were always one and the same."

"But how can you say that?"

"Because I knew her as both . . . unlike you."

Fern sat back in her chair, sympathetic to the confusion roiling in my head: *A mother who is once a wife-of-Christ paradigm.*

"As had your devoted mentor Ernest Ichabod Tyner."

Now she leaned forward and eyed me unflinchingly.

"Is he your father, Jeremiah?"

Rendered speechless, I began pacing the room. I had hoped her visiting me this night might have ended in a reconciliation between us. That we might lie alongside each other again . . . even in the innocent manner we had experienced in Alsada's dormitory. It was her body that I yearned to brush against mine again, its sudor to cloud my mind . . . her *petal of dusk* that tormented me.

Except reality had brusquely intruded.

"Why do you say that?" I cried. "Don't you think I know who my goddamn father is, Fern?"

"Not like I do mine," she countered, gesturing to the color of her skin.

"Unfortunately I can only point to my attraction for the woman you have become that connects me to the likes of Billy Coombs."

I sat back down and gathered myself before answering.

"Quite honestly, Fern, I've entertained that very question. *'Could Ichabod be my real father?'*"

"And?"

"Yes and no. Yes, because he and I are too much alike. We witness what occurs about us and comment on it. But we aren't actors. We're recorders."

"Why no?"

"Because I've returned to Berea on a mission."

Fern reached out, taking my hand in hers.

"It's why I'm here," she said. "At Ichabod's request. He wants you to reconsider if for no other reason than for his sake."

"I don't understand."

"He will explain. Give him some time, Jeremiah. It's the least you owe him."

She stood up to leave.

At that moment, I felt as if my chest was collapsing onto my lungs. Like Fern was standing over me, mocking my Whitebread overtures to make love to her while feigning the Billy Coombs's model of indifference to her feelings . . . the dueling conflicts of who I actually was.

Instead, I stood before her naked as each man chided the other. *Pick your Daddy!* They taunted. *Pick your Daddy!*

Fern stepped close . . .

"I came because of you, Jeremiah."

In the streetlight outside Billy Coombs's house, I watched her recede into night as she walked back to Ichabod's.

CHAPTER FIFTEEN

"The cosmic perspective does not come naturally to us small, Earth-bound bipeds corticed with tender self-importance."[xx]

Chester, Eva, and Onkel Jakob were lying in my bed, eagerly waiting for me to join them. Onkel appeared to be the most anxious. A white rose pinned to his nightshirt, he sat up and pointed his finger at me.

"So, after weeks if not months or even years, your black heart finally spoke. *How does it feel?* What else might we expect from the sanctimonious offspring of Billy Coombs?

"Permit me to prune your apple tree, Lili Marlene."

Vor der Kaserne
Vor dem grossen Tor
Stand eine Laterne
Und steht sie noch davor
So woll'n wir uns da wieder seh'n
Bei der Laterne wollen wir steh'n
Wie einst Lili Marleen
Wie einst Lili Marleen [17]

Chester guffawed. "Pour him another beer. Perchance he'll jig the Crucifix at the foot of our bed."

---

17 *In front of the barracks Before the giant gate There stands a streetlamp It's where we used to wait And if that streetlamp still burns bright We'll stand again beneath its light Like back then Lili Marleen Like back then Lili Marleen*

On the other side of me this night, Onkel Jakob chose to lie by himself. "Welcome, home," he whispered in my ear, accompanied by his cacophonous snorting.

"Jakob's blood runs cold in our veins," Eva muttered.

* * *

Once they fell off to sleep, I wandered back downstairs, and in the ink-black I sought to recreate my conversation with Fern. To what extent had our exchange—and the earlier one at Ichabod's—pulled back the curtain that my mentor was seeking refuge behind?

His *costume* I perceived not unlike my mother's.

It was she who brought the two men into my life.

I now wanted to know what may have occurred between them prior to my birth. Ichabod and Billy Coombs were the same age. Hannah, I'm guessing, was a year or two their junior . . . and fancied as an attractive, corkscrew-haired brunette, not loath to discourage the attention of either young man.

I recalled Ernest's saying my mother was his sister. For whatever his reason, this was an obvious lie. Yes, she and Ernest were Jews . . . but the real question was why had she radically converted to Catholicism and became a Sisters of Conscience novitiate?

Supposedly, given my absence from Berea, he had traveled to Alsada's boarding house in Portsmouth to keep tabs on me. *Except Fern revealed it was actually Hannah he wanted to learn about.* Just as he surely had from the moment he first laid eyes on her but a street away from his nemesis Billy Coombs.

At some point of this sleepless night, I began to empathize with Ichabod's fateful impotency. His unrequited yearning for a woman who now only existed in his febrile imagination. Was he tortured by her chaste bouquet as I had been the petal of dusk's, while my father reveled in deflowering the neighborhood lovelies alongside the quarry creek that coarse into Berea's twelve rivers?

I'd now come to suspect that Billy Coombs had avenged himself for being spurned years earlier when he assaulted Sister Bernadette that night in St. Andrews's chancel.

Hannah knew the contours of his heart. There were none. What was the shrouded reason she found herself lying alongside him that night on the creek bed? She had cottoned to what he desired from her. Perhaps even more than she was willing to imagine.

Was it any mystery why she willed to burn the garments he stripped off her body in exchange for a habit and a veil?

Yet here was Ichabod urging me to bury the will to kill his neighbor.

* * *

The following afternoon I sat across from Ichabod and Fern in his living room. That morning a note from her had been slid under the kitchen door. "Please meet with us around noon. Love, Fern."

But I wasn't about to misinterpret her handwritten "love" for anything more than it implied: *You and I are allies in this endeavor . . . period.*

My being holed up in Billy Coombs's house for several weeks had signaled Ichabod to draw Fern into his appeal that he feared had fallen on deaf ears. Billy's sleeping over the night I'd locked my bedroom door undoubtedly struck his and my father's alarm.

"Jeremiah, I have a confession to make to you."

"I already know what it is," I replied. "There is no need for you to apologize as I understand why."

He shot a worried glance at Fern.

"But he speaks to a deeper issue." She let moments pass. "There is much you don't know, Jeremiah. Listen to our friend."

The pain on Ichabod's face was palpably evident.

"At the very start I was attracted to her. Just as was he, one street over from us. Neither was it a secret to our unconnected circle of friends. Except Billy had something going for him: He *beguiled* her . . . and that something I lacked."

Ichabod caught my nod of recognition.

"But what do any of us understand about allure at that young age? What I did perceive, however, was Hannah's maturity. She comported herself as a young woman comfortable in her skin. Tacitly self-possessed unlike me, she was able to laugh at herself in situations that I made a concerted effort to shy away from. Whatever the reason she aroused me each day and into the night, it doesn't matter. And despite being painfully aware of how she lit up in your father's presence, it did nothing to quell my longing for her."

"Even when you heard?" I interrupted.

Ichabod challenged me. "What do you know, son?"

"Nothing more than being your student would cause me to surmise. One summer evening Hannah lay alongside Billy Coombs at the creek bed . . . our neighborhood's salacious rumors birthplace. Convenient that it was deep in *his* backyard."

Apparently I'd given him license to speak his heart . . . although it grew unsettlingly detached.

"Yes. The innuendoes flourished like head lice the next day. Hannah had lost all composure and by that night she knocked on my parents' door, asking to see me. We sat out on our back stoop. I'd never seen her distressed . . . or could even imagine her crying.

"'I gathered my clothes and ran off,' she sobbed. 'It didn't happen.'"

"A rage boiling inside me willed to strike: *'You tellin' me that Billy Coombs didn't fuck you? Is that right, Hannah?'* Instead, I allayed her trembling and muttered 'I believe you.'"

Fern turned to Ichabod. "We are conditioned as young women to play with fire."

I whimsically gestured to my sternum.

Ichabod continued. "Hannah knew there would be repercussions. She was haunted by it . . . by what he might do to exact retribution for being denied the gratification he believed his due. Following that incident, she became a different person. To me, to everyone who knew and liked her, Hannah withdrew . . . so much so that all of us who had heard about what occurred at the creek bed that night suspected their lovemaking had been consummated. And Billy did nothing to refute it.

"But our relationship took on a new life. She found solace in my presence and trusted me implicitly. We became the closest of friends."

"Beguiling died?" I asked.

"There was nothing we didn't share with each other."

"Was it an intimate affair?" Fern interjected.

"To the point of where each of us chose not to proceed. Yes."

At this vulnerable stage of his confession, he stood up and walked out the kitchen door and into his backyard. Fern uttered, "There's more."

Minutes passed before he returned to the room's cogent silence.

Sitting down, Ichabod rubbed his face with both hands as he appeared to catch his breath. He addressed me straight on.

"This is where it gets heavy. Perhaps too much so. You see, your mother and I were in love, Jeremiah. I was old enough now to understand that. But ours was doomed in that we'd never lie unclothed alongside each other as she had with Billy Coombs years earlier being she'd chosen Christ to be wedded to and not me.

"And we were both Jews!" He chuckled self-consciously.

"But *what* competition, wouldn't you say? It would be the Christians' Savior golden ring on Bernadette's fourth finger of her left hand and not my sixteen-carat one. Except it finally didn't matter to me. We were that close. I tended to exist in my imagination anyway. She understood that . . . another reason why I happily would have died for her.

"The truth is that I visited her numerous times in Springfield when she was a novitiate. We'd meet clandestinely and spend the chaste hours together. She would arrive at the hotel disguised in street clothes when we registered."

Ichabod paused as if he had anticipated my question.

"The Lafayette?"

"Most often."

You and she became one of Lionel's stories, I mused.

"Once she entered the convent and began taking her vows, each of us knew that we would no longer be able to be together as we had in the past. It's why she returned to Berea by bus that ill-fated day. That very night Billy Coombs slid down the pantleg of God and assaulted her in the chancel of St. Andrews, profaning a Jew in Christ's clothing at the foot of the plaster rood hanging high above their heads.

"Her cries in the sanctuary's smoke light unheeded while Onkel Jakob stood guard."

Distraught at this point, Fern and I looked inward. Ichabod had steeled himself, blankly reciting as though from another's memory.

"She was to leave from my place the following morning. Expecting her at any moment, I waited to bid her good night. Instead, appearing before me in the semidarkness of the living room, Hannah began removing her covenant garments. Within moments she approached me as if it were our wedding night.

"Mutely, she took me by my hands and trance-like led me up the stairs. She lay down on my bed, beckoning that I remove my clothes. I hesitated.

"'You must,' she replied. '*We have no choice.*' With dire finality, '*No choice.*'

"Her body limp and cold to the touch, she wept not of rapture but of grief, yet willfully drew me into her repeatedly. You may rightly question how this was ever possible. How was I, Ernest Tyner, to become her virile lover, given her unyielding embrace of despair?

"Summoning the countless nights in my imagination of our making love, I stood off to the side of our bodies rising and falling together. Then I heard her cry … just as she had in those concupiscent longings … '*It feels like water.*'

"That's when I knew. At daybreak Bernadette left to return to the convent."

Ichabod appeared to have momentarily fled his gaunt frame. The far-off look in his eyes spoke to neither Fern nor me. I believed it to be Hannah he was corresponding with. All I could envision was Gibby's wedding gown hanging forsakenly in Alsada's dormitory stairway.

He knelt beside me.

"Jeremiah, from that very day Billy Coombs brought you home from the hospital, and later when I saw you sunning outside in your crib on his front porch, I called you Son. So, now you know."

He hesitated.

"You have two fathers."

"But your devoted mother never let any doubt take root that it could be anybody but Billy Coombs who blighted the St. Andrews' chancel.

"Yet, among us three, let it be known that I never longed for Hannah's corporeal self any less than Billy did. My carnal reveries for years enabled me to enter sleep peacefully unlike the homilies of the Holy Scripture or as Fathers Tom and Jerry's sermons did.

"Was I not as guilty as my neighbor?

"I was Berea's Son of Christ, remember?"

"The recognition I received from the Padres on All Saints' Night . . . if they were mocking me, as I believe they might have been . . . I was the worthy target of their ridicule. Was I not the "holy" one of the Berea parish who caressed Hannah's petal-white breasts in my sweaty hands when I passed her house? Did I not breath the bouquet of ginger issuing between her thighs as a morning tonic? Who was carnally closer to Sister Bernadette than I? Not Billy Coombs. He thought only of himself when he penetrated a woman. Even when Hannah fled us in the rapid currents of the Mississippi, it was I, Ernest Tyner, who kept her alive in a manner that would cause the parish parishioners, especially the gentler sex, to turn beetroot red."

And prior to my leaving that day as I stood at his door, Ichabod gestured there was something else on his mind that he wanted to share. Unable to read his expression, I looked to Fern for direction. She too wore a mask of non-committal.

"I've expressed how close your mother and I were . . . even to the very end. I accompanied her to Little Egypt. The hazy skylight limning her body at the water's edge, she undressed before me. We embraced one final time.

"You, Jeremiah, hold dear a childhood memory of her in a red sacristy veil walking you through snowy woods.

"Mine is witnessing Hannah like she was seventeen years old shed her garments to skinny dip in the Big Muddy. I watched her stroke to its very center, then turn to glance back. Her lunar expression that once had set fire to Billy's and my ardor, now read bemused.

"Hannah drew her left arm out of the rapid current and waved before blowing me a mordant kiss.

"'*It feels like water,*' she cried as a baneful moon shadowed her downstream."

* * *

Ichabod's revelations that afternoon left me feeling mortally wounded. I wandered out of his house without uttering a word to either him or Fern. I had been erased from my story. The desire to requite her death was no longer anything other than a conceit to turn yet another page of my life. The scaffolding of self had collapsed.

Once back out on our street, I glanced at Billy Coombs's peeling white bungalow, laughing to myself thinking he was afraid to return home.

Because Orestes had murdered Clytemnestra to avenge his father's death?

I had become victim of my own storyline.

"*What are you afraid of, Jeremiah?*

"*Abandoning the plots you have already cribbed off our bookshelves to seek an identity. Are you that fragile?*" . . .

"*Look, we are the custodians of Jehovah's choir who sing off-key before falling into a dead sleep . . . parish bells with their clappers ripped out. Their cries of orgasmic release reverberate unanswered in our hallways.*

"If you wish to avoid madness, Jeremiah, never stray far from your desk."

That night in an untenanted room I dreamed that Onkel Jakob, outfitted in a Gestapo Uniform, had plucked my tongue, placing it in a tiny crystal bowl which he sat on the kitchen window sill.

"Watch it sprout, Jeremiah."

Virtually my life was owned by authors Ichabod and Billy Coombs. Its setting and place in time belonged to St. Andrews parish and the Berea neighborhood. What did Jeremiah have anything to do with it except taking his first breath from its air?

I was little more than a walk-on.

And now to consider that snuffing out my father would somehow mollify my being haunted by Hannah's stroking off to oblivion? Ten mourners at the Big Muddy's riverside reciting the Kaddish?

Onkel Jakob on its opposite bank cheering her on in German?

I walked up to the limestone quarry. As one of the many boys in our neighborhood, I once dove off the cliff overlooking the water, hoping to touch its bottom. But I lacked the reservoir of breath and shot back up to its surface. Perhaps that should have told me something early on.

There were no pearls in Berea.

Only failed pasts from which we wove threadbare narratives

Of which I had been inadvertently caught up in one.

Are there page-turners in St. Andrews's burial ground?

At the quarry's mouth, the origin of the creek that ran behind Billy's house, its current swift and roiled not unlike that which Hannah rode.

Chester had made a paper sailboat out of a war story and sailed past Eva's house.

Perhaps I could salvage my feeble attempt into a more sea-worthy dinghy to carry me downstream beyond Berea's twelve rivers and out to sea.

CHAPTER SIXTEEN

"Was I not as guilty as my neighbor?"

Ichabod's question resounded in my being like a matin bell.

Could it not be asked of me why I had set out to murder Billy Coombs? Is it not within one's conscience where the Furies live and battle? *Would I have not been killing myself, given that my father's blood runs within my veins?*

What did he grasp about tempting fate, provoking unintended tragedy in our lives, that my immaturity blinded me to?

I had rehearsed the act in my head countless nights upon returning to Berea. It would be Billy and me alone in our living room. I suffered no compunction inviting him to his own demise. He had to perceive its primal fury in my eyes . . . or fists that would take him down to beat him to death. He alone had spawned the evil child who had grown up to destroy him.

When he raped Hannah in St. Andrew's chancel, had he not foreseen conceiving the bile of vengeance in my callow heart?

Yet that was the enigma I was now encountering. Billy Coombs would not have lifted a hand to defend himself the evening of my act. As a deaf-mute he would have by preference succumbed. Ichabod said as much.

I understood this . . . but why was I determined to proceed?

As if prior to his act he had embraced the unspoken *blood begets blood* curse that *the dead pursue the living for revenge*, the heirloom of the house of humanity.

The stain that even a Christ could not erase.
A son beating himself to death on his father.

Paradoxically it was only in this instance that as I imagined him copping his last breaths did I experience his solicitous consent that I could only imagine coming from my deceased mother.

If I am unable to accept the dark pathologies of our fathers . . . *how do I proceed*?

* * *

For days as I roamed through the rooms of Billy's house, fevered, seeing his expression at every turn, acknowledging that he and I had awakened the inviolate that lingers in our unconsciousness from time immemorial. The recognition predated the liturgies intoned at St. Andrews by Fathers Fenn and Ricciardo.

Something darker had entered our lives. My locking the bedroom door that night when Billy returned home mocked how little I knew when I awakened the dead to pursue their grievances.

Billy's house had now become their residence. He and Ichabod understood of what I was incapable.

In my imagining beating him to death, why else would he not have defended himself if he hadn't heard the women upstairs with their black robes swirling and snakes in their hair taking occupancy?

It felt as if we had been stripped bare of our pretense of normality. That life as we understood it in Berea was nothing more than obfuscation. Designed perhaps by these darker forces to permit us humans to amuse our self with life and death, its joys and deep sorrows. Children who we were perceived to be. Why else, I thought, were Onkel Jakob, Chester, Eva, and now Gibby who had recently reappeared before me in her winding robe—the wedding dress—gathered about me for days on end with no sleep?

A testament to what each had already experienced . . . and, of course, I hadn't.

The deceased merely depart our perceived reality, I thought. The

Furies upstairs reveled in my naive hubris. The chthonic rite they performed among themselves made risible we "small, Earth-bound biped(s) corticed with tender self-importance."

Berea began to appear as a giant stage set designed to lull the living to believe they are.

Perhaps, I, Jeremiah, was nothing more than an actor in this drama the mythic deities had created for their entertainment. My naive righteousness had deceived me into believing I was self-determined, free to act on my own perception of reality. Wasn't it equally possible that I was nothing more than a stock character trundled out of storage when those gods became bored and, once again, wished to replay the cycle of vengeance drama when "the mortals overcome, insane to murder kin"?

Was I any more real than Onkel Jakob, Chester, Eva or Gibby—the dead who continued to visit me at will? Was Jeremiah the protagonist of a book written by another hand?

It was the daybreak following a sleepless night that I found him lying alongside me in bed. His self-mocking grin gave him away.

Of course, it's you, I thought. *It was only a matter of time until you revealed yourself. Did you come for the performance? The ladies are in the next room arranging the snakes in their hair . . . and adjusting their stygian robes.*

I was now free to separate myself from the individual who someone named. Was it Hannah's preference or possibly Billy's? Did it matter anymore than the arbitrary assigning of identities to characters in scripts or stories?

Turning to my right side, I said, "You couldn't have arrived at a better time, Jeremiah. The story is now yours. Congratulations. The Daughters of the Night will be overjoyed when they open our door."

* * *

At night locusts of guilt tore at Jeremiah's sleep. In daylight they blackened the windows, only to devour whatever food Onkel Jakob, Gibby, and their chorus mourners had placed before him. For it was a wake. He had become a witness to his own demise. Soon Ichabod would be knocking on the front door to pay his respects. Billy Coombs may possibly even stand outside on the porch with his head bowed as Eva recites the Kaddish.

But it was those rising voices of the black-clad women in the adjoining space, their hair now illuminated by glowing red eyes of the chthonic reptiles who terrified him.

> *Show us the mortals overcome,*
> *Insane to murder kin—we track them down*
> *Till they go beneath the earth,*
> *And the dead find little freedom in the end.*[xxi]

When Cronus, one of the twelve Titans, castrated Uranus or *Father Sky*, from Uranus's blood, which splattered onto the earth, came the Furies. Having learned about Greek mythology early on under Ernest Tyner's tutelage, young Jeremiah considered this yet another colorful anecdote from an unenlightened period in our history. Confessing his sins to remain in the graces of the *Father, Son,* and *Holy Ghost* appealed to him as a more rational and loving union with our creator.

Except the ancient women were now about to drive him mad while the tarnished crucifix above his bed was but a child's chimera should he die before he awoke.

* * *

However, the Daughters of the Night—their voices legion—had already occupied our room, yet only one approached the bed.

Jeremiah began to tremble.

"What is it?" I asked.

Then we saw: Eva Butter, mother-naked, cupped her right breast within inches of his face.

"Isn't this what you and your boyhood friends lusted after? Don't you recall?"

Cacophonous laughter reverberated throughout the house. Eva now sidled up close, beckoning each of us to lie in the raw alongside her. "Come, satisfy your yearning inside me."

I resisted the loins' tantalizing bouquet. Yet Jeremiah, aroused, reached out to suckle, but cried out, repulsed by a Star of David that glowed jaundice-yellow at its pulsing nipple.

Provoked once again, Billy Coombs's walls echoed those of a madhouse the instant luminous red-eyed serpents slithered from Eva's tangled hair to nest at his groin.

Berea's son grew deathly cold as Chester Grange and Onkel Jakob stood at our backyard window looking on.

"Don't abandon me," he pleaded. "You mustn't leave me alone."

But the chthonic reptiles had settled in. And Eva acted as if she were spent for the night.

I despaired hearing footsteps ascending the stairway, say, those of Fathers Fenn and Ricciardo to administer Jeremiah his last rites.

Just as when he was a child, and Bernadette was our mother, I knelt at the side of the bed and prayed.

While the goddesses of vengeance gathered under it awaiting sunup.

CHAPTER SEVENTEEN

"We want no part of their pious white robes—the Fates who gave us power made us free."[xxii]

I awoke to Billy Coombs standing outside my bedroom door, asking that I unlock it.

"Who's with you?"

"Onkel Jakob."

"If you have come to see your son, he is no longer here."

Jeremiah in a fetal position lay at my side, quaking at the sound of Billy's voice. "No need to worry," I whispered. "I won't let either of them hurt you."

"But he's my father."

"It's why he's here," I said.

I climbed out from under the comforters and unlatched the door. The women under our bed sounded like crickets from hell. By now I realized only Jeremiah and I could hear them.

Onkel Jakob's Nazi uniform was glazed saffron by the morning sunlight. Yet he wore his tap shoes, their leather scarred the flesh of an aged man.

"I've come to ask your forgiveness." Billy reached out his hand to me as the other traced the signs of the cross.

"Why? Because Jeremiah deigned to kill you?"

Stricken by the word, he visibly recoiled.

"You've come to the wrong place to seek absolution," I said. "Go instead where vicars Fenn and Ricciardo suffer no jurisdiction. Where the Daughters of Night mock confession boxes and incense thuribles . . . the pricks of conscience who deny sleep even to the dead from which even your Padres' Christ has not risen."

Billy Coombs's pallor abruptly turned cadaverous. Jeremiah stepped outside my shadow.

"You are no longer of any help to him, Billy. He lay in this very room days on end plotting bloodshed as the asps rained from the limbs of your barren apple tree.

"Onkel Jakob knows of what I speak."

Except he'd turned a deaf ear to my words. Like they no longer registered to him. His hands began to waver before his face as if to ward off insects attacking his eyes and cheeks.

Had the women under the bedstead begun to emerge?

Now, Jakob too. Maddened by gnats, he kept slapping his Nazi tunic.

"Seek forgiveness elsewhere, Father," I cried. "Circle Ichabod down St. Andrew's dooryard.

> *"A mighty god is Hades. There*
>   *at the last reckoning underneath the earth*
>   *he scans all,*
>   *he squares all men's accounts*
>   *and graves them on the tablets of his mind."xxiii*

"The boy you shed in Hannah's womb need not unsettle your sleep any longer as it was a mother's blood that gave him life."

"Yes, Jeremiah. But I, too, recall how dripping wet the hem of her red scapular had become from brushing the snow path. When she shut the door of this very room, the wet shadow of her lingering presence followed her outside like brush fire.

"Our attraction did not begin nor end at St. Andrews chancel, Jeremiah. Your craving my death would not have turned her scapular white."

When Billy reached out to embrace me, I declined but ushered our visitors down the stairs and out the backdoor.

Onkel Jakob strode far wide of the McIntosh stump, scanning the half-light for snakes writhing aloft in its vacant limbs.

* * *

Before nightfall, Jeremiah and I went into the living room to see if Ichabod was on the front porch, convinced he had wrung the doorbell. One long ring followed by a very short one. Both of us heard it. But when I opened the door, he wasn't there.

It wasn't like him not to show up, especially now. We walked out to the curb and looked up toward his house. Had Fern left?

Could they have traveled back to Alsada's boarding house, I wondered?

I turned to go back inside.

"Jeremiah, it's almost dark. I'm certain Ichabod will drop by in the morning. Come. Let's go to bed."

But he didn't move. He stood there peering up Cascade Street even when the sky turned pitch black.

For what felt like a full hour . . . I sat on the porch waiting.

Passing cars' headlights periodically traced his anguished mien.

By now I had begun to worry and went into the house to retrieve Billy's flashlight.

When I returned outside, Jeremiah had vanished.

I began to panic and cried out for him.

Except there were no echoes. Like the night had swallowed them.

The flashlight batteries offered little more than candlelight.

"Jeremiah!" I thundered. "We must go back inside."

I heard our kitchen door slam and ran into the backyard.

There, bathed in fading starlight, he stood with his arms reaching out to me.

"Come," he implored. "I don't want to go there alone."

He'd covered his head in Mother's veil, and in his hand, draped Bernadette's scapula.

"Help me put this on," he cried. "I don't want to go alone."

Only at that moment did I grasp what was occurring:

They were leaving me.

"No," I burst out. "This day's been too long. It's wearied you, Jeremiah. We must return inside."

But now in the fractured starlight he mirrored Mother standing there as if she had divorced herself from her body and mind. The cerise scapula as if tailored for presentation in a bier prior to her loved one's emerging. A private showing for Billy Coombs perhaps.

"How does it look, love?" he implored. "Hold me. For Christ's sake, touch me."

Then as if he were my brother, Jeremiah began to weep.

The pathos of his standing lifeless there, soiled in melancholia and despair, brought me to my knees.

"Oh, Jesus, no!" he cried. "Get up, you bastard." And he began laughing as if he'd spoken the truth.

Savagely he began to hurl the amputated limbs of Onkel Jakob's stillborn dream at Billy's house. One after another.

They pelted its clapboards like gun shots.

An outside light suddenly turned on in the neighbor's house.

Jeremiah froze.

"Come," I said. "We'll go down over the hill like we're circus vagabonds outfitted in our Saint's Day costumes."

Traveling on foot through the dark, we stopped at the quarry creek together.

Its starlit currents a broken mirror.

A sudden quietude began to wash over Jeremiah's expression. I even detected a nascent grin.

He turned facing me.

"This is where it all ends, doesn't it?" he asked.

"Tomorrow at sunup."

"Will she be present?"

"She was," I said.

* * *

Sleeping light that night, I awoke at dawn by the sound of tinkling brass bells that seemed to be coming from the bottom of our street. I glanced at Jeremiah who still lay sound asleep to my right. He looked angelically peaceful as newborns often do when not awake. Likewise his roseate lips hinted a wistful smile.

"This is where it all ends, doesn't it," surely had been his soporific.

Glancing out our bedroom window that framed only the house next door revealed nothing but parchment blinds pulled tight to its sills.

From Billy's bedroom panes I could make out what appeared to be a procession of sorts. Young and elders holding brass items that reflected the morning sun. But these were not band instruments. Instead it was a parade of holies, all males dressed in sundry shaded clerical garments. And a few of the men dangling brass pots on chains from which rose smoke.

What are they cooking? I mused.

Transfixed before Billy's window and empty bed—no Magdalena, her creampuffs nesting at her side—I witnessed the procession creep closer to our house.

Then I understood. It was not a replica of an All Saints' Day parade. Instead the St. Andrews' Padres Fenn and Ricciardo were soon to lay my *Other* down.

"Jeremiah!" I cried. "Wake up. We will soon entertain our company." Within seconds he stood naked in the doorway wiping sleep from his eyes. *Mon Dieu* . . . they were the iridescent liquid blue of Christ's! Instinctively, I began to chortle as did he. "Do you understand why I'm laughing? I asked.

"Yes. You said last night that it all ended today for me. *Why wouldn't I laugh?*"

"Please come to the window, Jeremiah."

He appeared to be disinterested by how slowly he strode to look out.

I sat on the bed and asked Jeremiah to describe what he was seeing.

"At the crest of the parade, Father Fenn is holding a brass pole—it must be at least eight feet tall—on top of which sits a wooden cross from which hangs a chalk-white Christ with crimson lips. And I swear there's a sun-halo over Jesus's head."

Jeremiah clearly was fixated on what was unfolding between us and the spectacle as it came closer to Billy's porch.

"Go on," I encouraged.

"Then behind Father Fenn is Father Ricciardo who's dangling what looks to be a small brass cooking pot with a lid. Except there's something cooking in it, for smoke is rising out of it as the padre sweeps it back and forth before him. His eyes blissfully closed like it's his favorite meal being prepared."

"It's called a Thurible," I said.

"What's inside?"

"Frankincense, Myrrh, wood, and cedar chips from over St. Andrew's *collino*[18]."

The bells had now become more pronounced.

"Jeremiah, tell me about the chimes. Whadaya see?"

"Sacristy bells. Don't you remember? You were once an altar boy."

I rolled over on Billy's bed and howled.

"Holy Christ, yes! I had to time their ringing exactly right or the priest would clip my head with the altar bell when the mass was over and we were alone. He called me a stupid shit so often I began to believe it."

"Four altar boys are tolling the brass bell sets in time to no music. That's strange. Yet they are ringing in unison. Wonder if they're counting Tom and Jerry's footsteps?"

By now I could tell the procession ceased moving directly outside the house.

"Go get dressed, Jeremiah."

---

18 hill

He stood staring at me with that half diabolical grin.

"Oh, yeah. Sure. What the fuck should I wear? My winding clothes?"

"Onkel Jakob will assist. Go back into our bedroom."

Then I heard a knock on our kitchen door.

Both Billy Coombs and Ernest Ichabod Tyner stood there solemnly outfitted in black tuxedoes. But neither wore a carnation boutonniere. Behind them sat the red Papal Chair on which Ichabod was once feted by the padres.

"Is he up?" Ichabod asked.

"Yes. He's upstairs with Onkel Jakob and I don't yet know who else."

"Let us know when we're to come in," Billy said.

Both men moved toward the MacIntosh stump as if it continued to provide shade from the brighter-than-usual morning sunlight.

Then the sacristy bells began to intone once again as the St. Andrews' procession strode into the backyard. I stood on the kitchen doorway stoop waiting to see the expression on Billy and Ichabod's faces.

None.

As if *everyone* had been informed.

Like it had all been written down even before Jeremiah was born.

The ceremony would be unique only to him it seemed.

It was all just a matter of when.

In his resplendent multicolored clerical garb, Father Fenn looked frozen in salt as he stood staring nowhere while gripping the brass rod on top of which perched the *Leonardo Baroque Processional Cross* that as a young altar boy had possessed me. It stood in a sacristy closet alone. Nailed above the sallow Christ's head on a snippet of gold ribbon were the black letters INRI. Until I was much older and inquired of Ichabod as to their meaning, I presumed they were an edict of sorts from Lucifer. They appeared to me more evil than even Jesus suspended from the wooden cross's arms, his hands and feet pinioned there for time eternal by three-penny spikes.

Both priests cautioned me to never touch the processional cross or dare even to stare at it.

"Why do you think it's in the closet alone?" they would caution when I'd inquire about it.

Father Fenn always wore white gloves on the few occasions he would expose it to the light of day.

I studied him now, waiting for Jeremiah to appear.

His white gloves were wringing with sweat . . . just as the hem of Hannah's red scapula absorbed water.

St. Andrews's church bells began to peal. Yet, it was Saturday morning not Sunday. Never had this occurred in my lifetime. They pealed eight times.

Every person in the procession, including the two blood fathers, turned their attention to Billy Coombs' kitchen door.

To my utter surprise outstepped Gibby in the very outfit she wore to escape the white hoods the morning she climbed out of the open sewer on DeForest Road. She was jubilantly humming "Nearer My God To Thee," the hymn cousin Bennie had played on his Hammond B-3.

She's setting the mood, I thought . . . *the Second Line parade mood*.

The altar boys sacrilegiously rang the sacristy bells in perfect time. Their black patent-leather shoes counterpointed the rhythm.

"Jeremiah will be thrilled," I thought.

Chester Grange followed, wearing his Marine lieutenant's dress uniform. Pinned to his chest were various harmonica replicas instead of military ribbons and brass marksmanship buttons. The one that mirrored the morning sun the most was his beloved silver Chromonica.

Behind him stood young Eva who never enjoyed being alive beyond her fifteenth birthday. She wore the swimming suit the day in which she drowned after being swallowed alive by Berea's Municipal Park pool draining pipe that flowed into the Neshannock River.

The cloth cup of the upper left part of her two-piece garment had been ripped out, exposing the Star of David tattoo in place of her pubescent breast's nipple. Unlike the other participants gathered, Eva looked under psychic distress.

But then time had suddenly iced over. There was no wind, no shadows, no jingling bells, no restless fidgeting among the gathering.

Like the *Cinema Paradiso*'s projector had jammed.

We all stood there waiting for what we had been programmed centuries earlier to expect.

And that's when the appearance of Onkel Jakob, resplendent in his SS uniform, with a black buckled belt at his uniform's midriff, and his riding jodhpurs puffed out at his thighs like ravens' wings, complemented by black mirror-leather boots that rose to his knees. Once he stepped upon the kitchen stoop, we were all put on notice that he tap-danced when out of costume.

Onkel's cleats rapped the concrete like brass high-tops when struck.

Order between the living and the already dead had been established: Padres governed the parish denizens . . . and Onkel Jakob rode herd over the hapless ghosts.

Jeremiah's and our family all.

Onkel gestured to Billy Coombs and then to Ichabod. Beckoning them to enter the house with the red papal chair.

Now it all began to take on the trappings of an established ritual. The two men, not unlike those who pass the collection plates from pew to pew each St. Andrews's Sunday with deliberate finality, Billy and Ichabod deftly marched in time with the chair into Billy's house.

Only one person was missing now.

Unsurprisingly, at least to me, a dark rain cloud shrouded the sun when Billy and Ichabod—the two blood fathers—carried Jeremiah outside. He sat upright in the red papal chair outfitted in Gibby's wedding gown, his appointed winding sheet.

His inscrutable expression signaled to neither the dead or alive factions.

At that moment, the bells began sounding alive again, the censor pot proceeded boiling the frankincense and myrrh, Father Fenn's procession cross animated when the sun quickly returned, and Gibby in mourning weeds bombinated "Nearer My God To Thee" as we all strode down over Billy's backyard *colline* to the quarry creek.

Berea's Second Line was jubilantly alive once again until the procession stopped dead at the narrow water's edge.

In unison the assembled lowered their heads as no one wished to behold what we knew was about to happen next.

I could hear muffled sobs in the crowd. The four altar boys sounded like girls crying.

Even Onkel Jakob choked up when he attempted to request the padres to give the Sign of the Cross as Jerimiah's fathers laid him down, shrouded in Gibby's wedding gown, into the gelid quarry runoff.

On the left side of the creek Father Fenn spoke, while opposite him Father Ricciardo waved the smoking Thurible.

> *"Faithful God,*
> *Lord of all creation,*
> *you desire that nothing redeemed by your Son*
> *will ever be lost,*
> *and that the just will be raised up on the last day.*

> *Comfort us today with the word of your promise*
> *as we return our brother to the waters."*

Onkel Jakob was now on his knees clutching Jeremiah from rushing off to his wedding.

Padre Ricciardo uttered the final homily.

> *"Grant Jeremiah Coombs a place of rest and peace*
> *where the world of dust and ashes has no dominion.*
> *Confirm us in our hope that he will be created anew*
> *on the day when you will raise him up in glory*
> *to live with you and all the Saints*
> *for ever and ever.*
> *Amen"*

When Onkel Jakob stood up, all of the present, living and deceased, witnessed Jeremiah embraced by the quarry currents as he slowly disappeared from our collective vision. We all were aware from childhood of how the creek ran under the street in a series of tunnels and gigantic concrete culverts clear to the twelve Berea rivers in town. It didn't matter which one by chance he was directed to as they all eventually headed straight into the Ohio toward the Big Muddy *a.k.a.* the *Gathering of Waters*.

I was the last one to head back to Billy's house where Eva had prepared a buffet for the assembled. Chester Grange sat out alone on the McIntosh stump, smoking.

I asked him what he planned to do now that it was all over.

"Don't know," he replied. "How about you?"

CHAPTER EIGHTEEN

At dusk, shadows began to shroud the Coombs' domain. All the activity surrounding Jeremiah's watery send-off hours earlier had dissipated. Even the neighborhood lingerers who stood watching from their front porches long after the St. Andrews procession filed back to the parish grounds had turned in.

Billy's house looked abandoned.

Gingerly turning the backdoor's latch, I cried "Hello."

No reply.

Once inside the kitchen, I called out for Billy and Ichabod, hoping they were awaiting me in the living room. But even the echoes came back muffled as if the rooms had been empty of any activity for months . . . or more. Thin sheets of dust enveloped the Formica table and chrome chairs. The gas stove cast-iron burners looked chalky-white with stopped-time bloom.

Even the dwelling's memories had vacated its dead air.

The living room's overstuffed chair and sofa manifested no sign of an occupant's posterior imprint.

I laughed to myself—I swear I heard it reverberate in the kitchen—pondering if the deceased left trails. If perchance they made love, say, on a bloodred sofa, would the velvet lime their bodies?

I cried out again. "Fern?"

But nobody answered. Unnerved of going up the stairs for fear of what I might encounter, I reclined on the sofa and watched the room slowly turn night-black . . . save the amber streetlight outside the house casting its wind-flicking shards to gambol about on the living room's walls.

Would Ichabod stop by? I mused. *How about Billy?*

My two fathers who started it all . . . had they left their story behind? Inside a veneered walnut wardrobe upstairs in Billy's bedroom hung a blue seersucker two-piece suit along with a polka-dot bow tie, and underneath a pair of brown and white spectator wingtips . . . his mockery of summer. Alongside, one drawer of yellowing cotton briefs.

They felt entombed to me. I could hear the suit jacket whimper for a lake-side breeze, the bouquet of young women, the syncopation of lyric fireflies illuminating the darkness.

Yet his bed appeared as if a body had once lay there undetected for time indeterminate because it buckled at its center as would a dead man . . . or woman. We leave our indelible marks as trails.

Billy's house memorialized them this night.

Had he died? I wondered. *"Had Billy Coombs perished?"*

A car passing outside the house, its headlights joined the street-light to race about the walls in a feverish cavort.

And then I recalled:

When Billy passed away I chose not to attend the open-casket showing, thinking Ernie Tyner might pay his last respects. I feared witnessing my father reach out to latch onto the man's rayon tie, hoisting himself up to his friend's torso, and Ichabod, surprised not in the least, turning to me, winking, and saying, "Follow us, kid. I know an old Ukrainian hall outside Stroudsville. I'll whirl him about in the darkness for a while, then . . . it'll be your turn. But you gotta hold Billy tight. He tends to slide down your legs.

"Make sure you fan your arms out same as a whooping crane, and if you get the urge to trumpet like one into the inky light of the armory . . . Christ yes, just do it, 'cause all these other souls are sleeping, son. Eternally sleeping."

That's what I was dismayed of not seeing.

I couldn't brook watching the priest close the lid on Billy Coombs's seraphic ruse, his dancing shoes.

> *Or accepting that only the bus-full of the dead return home at dusk.*
> *Or believing that when night closed in on me—the carriage idling outside my doorway—Billy wasn't going to wrap himself about me, murmuring . . .*
> *Circle wide, boy. Circle wide. The floor is all ours.*

At daybreak, I watched Ichabod step out of his bungalow and head down our street to the bus stop. I rushed out onto the porch to greet him. It had been too long as I yearned to have him call me "Son" and invite me to resume our Lessons of life in his diminutive basement theater. I longed to begin exchanging ideas and books with him, those he carried each night on his trip back home from the pottery.

The parchment Christ of our Cascade Street, the light that had escaped the refuse-filled quarry, its immutable smoke, the closed wooden and iron-hinged doors of St. Andrews . . . the Ichabod of Time who made my heart beat in spite of the Parish's wooden bells and brass priests of eternal suffering and doom. Our daily bread.

"*Mon Dieu,* Ichabod!" I wailed, running out onto the street to grab hold of his hawser-like frame. And laughed heartily like I'd risen from the dead . . . planted all about us like dogwood trees.

And when I clutched his body I felt only a wisp of air.

As if I had banged into him with a red bumper car, his wind gusting back into my face.

"Oh, Jesus! I'm sorry, dear friend. *Father.* It's just that I've been afraid I'd never see you again . . . and I longed to die. But now you are here. Allow me to accompany you to the bus stop and we'll make plans for nightfall. Okay?"

Except there were no dodgems. There was no Norman armory's cavernous assembly hall where a Wurlitzer cast rainbow lights onto its deserted stone floor.

Ichabod never heard me. I was no longer there.

He and his friend Billy had officiated the send-off of Jeremiah to the Big Muddy in Bernadette's wake.

It was sufficient in the scheme of life.

Mother and Son.

Standing outside my father's house which would soon go up for sale, I watched him signal Ichabod to hurry for the bus was arriving. As Billy stepped in, he turned and assisted Ernie Ichabod Tyner to hop on.

I wandered down to the tunnel that lay under the bottom of our street and through which the quarry creek flowed, hoping to discover some evidence that Jeremiah had sailed inside it onto Berea's downtown. A tangled outgrown of common reed and milkweed plants occluded its opening. Making my way downward to the rapid current, I peered inside the child-tall culvert. And there but an arm's length away on a wayward hickory branch hung Hannah's Sisters of Conscience frayed white headscarf.

I gently freed it and pressed it to my face.

It felt like water.

ENDNOTES

i *Jonah's Gourd Vine*, Zora Neale Hurston, Novels and Stories, The Library of America, Ch. 11, pp 30

ii African American Proverb

iii *Cane*, Jean Toomer, Norton Critical Second Edition, "Kabnis," pp 83

iv African American Spiritual

v Traditional African American Work Song

vi *Their Eyes Were Watching God*, Zora Neale Hurston, Novels and Stories, The Library of America, Ch. 13, pp 279

vii *Cane*, Jean Toomer, Norton Critical Second Edition, "Blood-Burning Moon," pp 33

viii *Their Eyes Were Watching God*, Zora Neale Hurston, Novels and Stories, The Library of America, Ch. 1, 175

ix *Cane*, Jean Toomer, Norton Critical Second Edition, "Bona and Paul," pp 78

x Ibid, "Carma," pp 14

xi *Jonah's Gourd Vine*, Zora Neale Hurston, Novels and Stories, The Library of America, Ch. 26, pp 168

xii Matthew 19:14 KJV

xiii *Cane*, Jean Toomer, Norton Critical Second Edition, "Avey," pp 45

xiv *K*, Roberto Callasso, Knopf, Ch. I, pp 4

xv Ibid, Ch. I, pp 18

xvi Ibid, Ch. II, pp 40

xvii *The Castle,* Franz Kafka, Reading Essentials, 2019, Ch. 1, pp 19

xviii *K*, Roberto Callasso, Knopf, Ch. IV, pp 90

xix *Cane*, Jean Toomer, Norton Critical Second Edition, "Bona and Paul," pp 78

xx *The Marginalian.org*, Maria Popova, 07.25.2021

xxi *The Eumenides*, Aeschylus, Penguin Classics, pp 246

xxii Ibid, pp 246

xxiii Ibid, pp 270

BIOGRAPHICAL NOTE

Dennis Must is the author of four novels: *MacLeish Sq.* (Red Hen Press, Nov. 2022), *Brother Carnival* (Red Hen Press 2018), *Hush Now, Don't Explain* (Coffeetown Press 2014), and *The World's Smallest Bible* (Red Hen Press 2014); as well as three short story collections: *Going Dark* (Coffeetown Press 2016), *Oh, Don't Ask Why* (Red Hen Press 2007), and *Banjo Grease* (Creative Arts Book Company 2000; Red Hen Press 2019). He won the 2014 Dactyl Foundation Literary Fiction Award for *Hush Now, Don't Explain*; in addition, he was a finalist in the 2019 Next Generation Indie Book Awards for *Banjo Grease*, the 2016 International Book Awards for *Going Dark*, and the 2014 USA Best Book Award in Literary Fiction for *The World's Smallest Bible*. His plays have been produced off-off-Broadway and has been published in numerous anthologies and literary journals. During his long life, he was a member of the Author's Guild and resided in Salem, Massachusetts from 2001 until his death in 2024.